CHRIS CRUTCHER

Deadline

Deadline

GREENWILLOW BOOKS
An Imprint of HarperCollinsPublishers

This book is a work of fiction. References to real people, events,
establishments, organizations, or locales are intended only to provide
a sense of authenticity, and are used to advance the fictional narrative.
All other characters, and all incidents and dialogue, are drawn from
the author's imagination and are not to be construed as real.

Deadline
Copyright © 2007 by Chris Crutcher
All rights reserved. No part of this book may be used or reproduced
in any manner whatsoever without written permission except in
the case of brief quotations embodied in critical articles and reviews.
For information address HarperCollins Children's Books,
a division of HarperCollins Publishers, 1350 Avenue of the Americas,
New York, NY 10019.
www.harpercollinschildrens.com

Printed in the United States of America
The text of this book is set in Glouces Old Style MT.
Jacket photograph © 2007 by Edyta Pawlowska
used under license from Shutterstock, Inc.

Library of Congress Cataloging-in-Publication Data
Crutcher, Chris.
Deadline / Chris Crutcher.
Greenwillow Books.
 p. cm.
Summary: Given the medical diagnosis of one year to live, high school
senior Ben Wolf decides to fulfill his greatest fantasies, ponders his life's
purpose and legacy, and has dream conversations
with a spiritual guide known as "Hey-Soos."
ISBN: 978-0-06-085089-0 (trade bdg.)
ISBN: 978-0-06-085090-6 (lib. bdg.)
[1. Terminally ill–Fiction. 2. Self-perception–Fiction.
3. High schools–Fiction. 4. Schools–Fiction.] I. Title.
PZ7.C89De 2007 [Fic]–dc22 2006031526

First Edition 10 9 8 7 6 5 4 3 2 1

 Greenwillow Books

In memory of you, Ted Hipple.
You treated our work with such respect,
and stood like a giant against the censors.

One

My plan was to focus my senior year on information I could use after graduation when I set out for Planet Earth from the Pluto that is Trout, Idaho, population 943. My SATs said I wasn't even close to brain-dead and I was set to be accepted at any college I chose, as long as I chose one that would accept me. A lot of guys use their senior year to coast; catch up on partying and reward themselves for making it this far. Not me. This was my year to read everything I could get my hands on, to speak up, push myself and my teachers to get the true hot poop on the World At Large, so I could hit the ground running. How big a pain in the ass do you think that would make me in Mr. Lambeer's U.S. government/current events class, where Lambeer regularly alters reality with the zeal of an evangelical senator?

I also intended to shock the elite by etching my name atop the winner's board at the state cross-country meet, then come home to take Dallas Suzuki by surprise. Dallas Suzuki may sound to you like a car dealership in Texas, but for the past three years, she has been the single prey in the crosshairs of my Cupid's bow, and she doesn't know it because she is way, way out of my league.

Mr. Ambitious.

Then, about two weeks after my eighteenth birthday, a month and a half before beginning my final year at Trout High, I discovered I'll be lucky to be there at the finish. A warning like that usually comes from the school office, to be ignored until the third notice, but this was from The Office Above The Office and was to be attended to immediately.

Doc Wagner left a phone message a few days after my routine cross-country physical; he wanted to see me with my parents in his office either ASAP or pronto. There was *gravity* in his voice, so I decided I'd better scout ahead to see if his message was PG-13 and suited for all, or R-rated and just for me. Turned out to be X.

"Hey, Ben," he said as he passed me in the waiting room. "Where are your folks?"

"Hey, Ben," he said as he passed me in the waiting room. "Where are your folks?"

"They couldn't make it."

"I'd really prefer they were here."

"My mom's . . . well, you know my mom; and Dad's on the truck."

"I'm afraid I have to insist," he said.

"I'll relay the information. Promise."

He said it again. "I'm afraid I *have* to insist."

"Insist all you want, my good man," I said back. "I'm eighteen, an adult in the eyes of the election board and the Selective Service and your people, the American Medical Association. I decide who gets the goods on yours truly." Dr. Wagner has known my family since before I was born and was plenty used to my smart-ass attitude. He's delivered probably 80 percent of the town's population my age and under, including my brother, and I'm not even close to his worst work. He also delivered Sooner Cowans.

"I don't feel right talking about this without your parents, Ben," he said, walking me toward the examination room. "But I guess you leave me no choice."

"I leave you exactly that," I said. "Lay it on me."

And lay it on me he did, and I am no longer quite so glib.

He sat on the stainless-steel swivel stool, a hand on my knee, staring sadly.

I said, "You're sure about this, right? There's no doubt?"

"There's no doubt. I sent your tests to Boise and they sent them to the most reputable clinic in the country. We can run them again, but unless your blood was mixed with somebody else's—and yours is the only blood I took that day—it's pretty much a lock. We have to get right on it. Otherwise you'll be lucky to have a year."

Doc took another blood sample, to be sure. I watched him mark it, but I knew the original tests were mine.

"Okay," I said, rolling down my sleeve. "Lemme sit with this a minute, all right?"

He hesitated.

"You got no sharp instruments in here, Doc, and nothing to make a noose. Go," I said, fighting the urge to let him stay. That's my curse: give me the bad news and I'll take care of *you*. I thank my mother for that.

Doc rose, and he looked old. He stood at the door, watching me over the top of his glasses, the cliché of a small-town doctor. The door closed behind him and I stared out the window, letting his words settle into my chest. *Otherwise you'll be lucky to have a year.*

The leaves of an ancient cottonwood outside the window danced in the bright sunlight, and I was breathless. I sat, digesting the indigestible, adrenaline shooting to my extremities as if I were strapped to an out-of-control whirling dervish. I was thinking of my mom. How in the world do I tell her this?

All my mother ever wanted was to be a good mother and a good wife, but that's not as easy as it sounds—for her at least—because she's crazy. She's either moving at warp speed or crashed in her room with the shades pulled. No gears in between. She calls herself a stay-at-home mom, but when she does stay at home, it's all you can do to get her out of her locked bedroom, and when she's not at home, she could be at the Chamber of Commerce or the Civic Club or any of a number of bridge or book clubs.

When Cody and Dad come home to a dark house, Mom's door closed tight like that of a dungeon, they pretend she's on vacation. I'm the one who tries to get in and make her feel better. File that under Don Quixote. Dad has his own bedroom because he's not willing to sleep on the couch during those long stretches of nights when her bedroom door is locked. He runs his mail and freight business like a fine Swiss clock, reads voraciously, and helps Cody and me problem solve, by request only. His demeanor doesn't change whether Mom is on fire or doused. His keel is as even as hers is tilted; it's kind of like living with roommates who are foreign exchange students from opposite points on the globe. I speak both their languages, while Cody speaks neither, and I spend way more time than I should translating. I knew even before I thought it all out that bringing them Doc's news would break the fragile symmetry of our lives. And, Oh God, what about my brother?

But I have to say, and this will sound strange, the minute Doc said it, I felt a *congruence.* I've never pictured myself over twenty; never really thought I would be. I've had this dream since grade school. This kid is in a hospital bed surrounded by doctors, nurses, and parents. Tubes protrude from his nose and he is seriously puny, and the only dialogue is, "It isn't working. It isn't working." I can't see that the kid's face is mine, but one of the people standing around the bed is my brother, Cody, and tears stream down his face. It's as if the universe slipped a long time ago and revealed to me my destiny.

So Doc left me to sit there and I betrayed him, but only a little bit. I left a note saying, "I'll be back. Don't worry. Won't do anything stupid." Then I drove home, put on my running gear, and headed out. I snagged my iPod because I had challenged myself to run through more than thirty-five hundred songs before the summer was out, so I could show up for cross-country in primo condition, and I didn't want to get caught running without polishing off some tunes.

I was five miles into it, standing on a high bluff in the shimmering heat, when I heard in my phones:

If life is like a candle bright
Then death must be the wind.
You can close your window tight
And it still comes blowing in

So I will climb the highest hill
And I'll watch the rising sun
And pray that I won't feel the chill
'Til I'm too old to die young.

I didn't remember downloading it, and didn't know who was singing, and technically it wasn't a perfect fit. But that old dream and this song merged to tell me the breeze whispering against my soft cotton shirt was death.

I walked back through the entrance to the county hospital dripping in sweat and asked Myrna

Whitney at the reception desk for Doc.

"Doc's been looking all over for you, Ben. Where in the world did you go? And look at you." She crinkled her nose.

Back in the examination room, Doc unloaded when I told him we weren't going to do anything about this. "That's the craziest thing I've ever heard! What in hell is wrong with you, Ben Wolf? You don't hear information like this and just give up! Now get on your phone and call your dad. I know this might be too much for your mother, but your dad is the most levelheaded man I know."

"And I want to keep him that way, Doc. Look. I know this doesn't make sense, but–"

"'Doesn't make sense' isn't the expression for it. It's stupid. And it's dangerous."

"But I've known this . . . maybe forever. I was never meant to grow old, Doc. I can't explain it. . . . "

"Well, when you can, explain it to someone who believes in voodoo. Don't explain it to me, 'cause I'm not listening. Now get on that phone with your dad."

"I'm eighteen, Doc. This is my call. I don't expect you to understand, but you have no choice but to go along. This shit is confidential."

Doc stormed into the hall, then back into the room before the door could close. "Ben, you might be eighteen, but you're a boy. If you stick with this ridiculous decision long, it will be too late to change your mind."

"I don't think I'm going to change my mind."

This time he stormed out for good.

Mid-August

"Get in." Doc opened the door to his twenty-year-old Chevy station wagon in front of my house. He'd called the night before and told me to be ready at five thirty A.M.; didn't say for what.

"What do I tell my dad?" I'd asked.

"Whatever you want."

"Where we going?" I asked now.

"Denver."

"Colorado?"

"Do you know another Denver?"

He was quiet on the drive to the airport, and through check-in and security, but on the plane he said, "Ben, I can't shoulder this alone. I'll go along with your decision, even though I wouldn't think twice about breaking confidentiality. I'm not afraid of the legal team you might throw together." He rolled his eyes to let me know what a joke that was. "But you know your family situation, I guess, and this is serious stuff."

I said, "Thanks. Really."

"Yeah, 'thanks'," he said. "But no thanks. I'm taking you to someone who can put this to you in the clearest terms. Like I said, I can't shoulder this alone."

The cab ride from the airport to the clinic just outside Denver was a blur, as was most of my time inside. We met with a young Indian doctor—like India-Indian—named Dr. Bachchan. In just a little bit of an accent she laid it out for me. That part was just as much a blur as had been the cab ride. I heard "aggressive," "resilient" (as applied to the disease, not me), "urgent," and "we haven't had much luck so far."

I walked away understanding I have a rare form of whatever the hell it is and without treatment my chances sucked, but with it they still sucked and somehow I knew my chances aren't about living, they're about living well. I wouldn't recommend this for anyone else, but I'm not going out bald and puking. I don't have anything to teach anyone about life, and I'm not brave, but I'd rather be a flash than a slowly cooling ember, so I'll eat healthy food, gobble supplements, sleep good, and take what the universe gives me.

And I'm turning out for football.

Two

Coach Banks stands near the center of the gym in his gold T-shirt (which is really yellow) and purple shorts behind two boxes of new shoulder pads, whistle dangling from his neck on a purple-and-gold lanyard, clipboard in one hand, purple-and-gold Cougar pen in the other, checking off names as each veteran player selects his armor. Todd Langford, the assistant coach, passes out knee and thigh pads and helmets. Freshmen and other first-year players sit in the bleachers, patiently waiting for the gear to be picked over, predicting individual heroics unlikely to be fulfilled. I slip into the bleachers while Cody checks in with Coach. A few vets look at me in surprise and wave, surely wondering why a senior who probably weighs five more pounds than his pads is turning out for football for the first time. Cody points me out to Coach, who removes his purple Cougar baseball cap, peers into the bleachers, shakes his head, and waves. I wave back.

It feels strange to pick up my gear with the frosh, but I'm enough smaller than most of *them* that we don't reach for the same set of shoulder pads at the same time. In fact there have been so few guys my size turning out for Cougar football in the past ten years that my ancient pads are barely used. I tuck them and my practice uniform into my gear bag and take a seat beside my brother. The Wolf brothers are both seniors, though I'm eleven and a half months older. Mom and Dad held me back a year, hoping I'd grow enough to look less like a *Wizard of Oz* extra by the time I started kindergarten, but to no avail, so I'm old for our class and Cody's young. Except that I'm approximately three quarters his size, we could be twins. Same general body design—plus or minus some muscles—same features, same hair and eyes. When he took over at quarterback in midseason last year and averaged five touchdowns, running or throwing, in the final five games they started calling him Big Wolf. Guess who that made me.

Coach paces in front of the bleachers. "I've been

giving the same speech more than fifteen years, so you vets feel free to sing along. Rooks best pretend you're hearing the audio version of the Bible for the first time; read by the protagonist."

A murmur runs through the crowd and Coach says, "I guess that would require a big 'Yes SIR!'"

In unison we roar, "Yes SIR!"

Coach smiles and takes off the cap again. "Almost makes me wish I'd been in the military," he says. "That's the last time I want to hear anyone calling me sir, got that?"

The freshmen and new guys, myself excluded, thanks to Cody, repeat, "Yes SIR!" while the veterans laugh.

"Gentlemen," he says, "football is a game. Many of the good citizens of Trout will tell you it's much more than that, but it's not a microcosm of life; it's not a religious or patriotic experience. It's a game. It's a hell of a good one, though, and if you hang in there you'll get to play. You'll ride the bench until I think you can help us, but you won't get cut, and the more effort you put in and the more carefully you listen—and put into practice what you hear—the better are your chances of extended playing time. Understood?"

There were fewer "Yes SIR!"s this time, more grunts of agreement.

When Sooner Cowans heard "SIR!" he sneered, like he couldn't believe the dumb shits he was going to be playing with.

"By now you've all signed off on the school's Athletic Code. It demands no drinking, no drugs, and no smoking for all in-season athletes. It also requires that you report those behaviors on other in-season athletes should you gain firsthand knowledge of their participation in them. You're also aware of our school's general zero-tolerance policy on drugs, alcohol, and violence." He scans the bleachers.

We nod and grunt.

Sooner's glare sweeps the bleachers, practically daring anyone to lay zero-tolerance anything on him.

"You can give me 'Yes!'" Coach says. "It's the 'sir' I don't like."

So we yell "Yes!"

"Well, I'm not a detective and I don't demand you rat out your buddies. It sets you up to be liars and me to be lied to and I have no time for that. I pay attention to performance. If you're drinking it will affect your performance. If you're using drugs it will affect your performance. If you're causing violence in school you'll get suspended or expelled and you'll be gone and there won't be any performance. I will not throw you off this team for your actions off the football field. I will, however, adjust your playing time in accordance with your actions *on* the football field.

"On the field, I expect you to give it your all, all the time. You owe that to your teammates and to yourselves; and to Coach Langford and me. Learn your plays; hit hard and hit clean. If I have an *inkling* that you're hitting to injure, in practice or in a game, I will jerk you off the field so fast your pads will remain at the point of infraction and, though I said football is not a religious experience, we will have a 'Come to Jesus' meeting in which I will play Jesus. We do not go after heads and we do not go after knees. This is a tough, high-risk sport and we will not add to that risk. Is that clear?"

"YES!"

"Beyond that, we hit to rattle skeletons."

Coach tosses his hat toward the nearly empty boxes of pads and removes his whistle. He sighs. "Fourteen years ago a boy named Ron Ingalls tried to hang himself in the athletic equipment room. Ron wasn't much of an executioner and I don't think he was all that serious because he knew I was coming and he left the light on and turned the radio up. When I got him down he said he did it because of the way the jocks treated him, and he named them. Every athlete he named played ball for me. It wasn't all jocks, guys, it was football players. Ron Ingalls was alone; not a part of anything.

"I teach English here, but in fact, I'm a scientist. What I know about science is that everything from the smallest atom to the universe itself works because of its *parts*. This team is a single entity. It works when everyone does his part, from the manager to the quarterback. I know, because I *know,* there are guys on this team who have nothing but contempt for other guys on this team. Off the field, hate away. On the field we *need* each other. Every one of us operates better when every player does his job. And understand this: if not for fans, you guys would be out on a dusty vacant lot with pieces of your mothers' old torn-up pillowcases tucked into your belts, playing flag football when there's nothing good on TV. The fans are part of this entity, too." He leans forward. "This is where Ron Ingalls comes in; every kid who walks the halls of Trout High is a member of this team. Do not be giving *any* members of the team a hard time, because I consider that to be detrimental to our mission and I will bench you so hard you'll be picking wood slivers out of your colon. Are there any questions?"

There are none.

"Okay," he says, "let's head for the cafeteria and get this first day of practice under our belts."

"Oh, and gentlemen," Coach says as we begin to clear the bleachers. "Some of you may have taken history or civics classes that outlined the freedoms one enjoys in a democracy. At the heart of those freedoms is *choice.* At this moment you have the freedom to choose whether or not to play football. With an affirmative choice, all democracy vanishes."

It's another two weeks before school starts, so we walk through darkened, deserted halls toward the cafeteria, where we come upon card tables covered with tablecloths, a candle burning in the center of each. Caterers from Lindemann's, Trout's best imitation of an upscale restaurant, wait to serve us our choice of soup, salad, a meat or veggie entrée, and a generous selection of desserts. This is one of Coach Banks's more eccentric traditions, marking our last day of relative comfort.

I'm the only guy who orders the veggies.

Coach squats next to Cody, who's sitting across from me. Randy Dolven and Rich Glover sit to my right and left, popping bite-size sirloin tips like popcorn. "Ben Wolf," Coach says. "This is your last year of high school.

You were headed for State in cross-country. What in hell are you doing here?"

"I want a new experience."

He can't help but take in my size. People I've never met do that the moment they hear my deep voice and realize I'm not a sixth grader, but I've known Coach since junior high school when he came to our house to lay out future plans for my brother, took a look around, and turned into our backup dad. In Coach's defense, he *is* seeing me for the first time, in this light. "The new experience could be brain damage," he says.

Dolven says, "That wouldn't be a new experience."

"Have you talked with Coach Gildehaus?" Coach asks. Gildehaus coaches cross-country.

"I left a message on his answering machine yesterday afternoon," I say. "I'll talk with him today."

"He called Coach Gildy when he knew he wouldn't be there," Cody says, "like I do with you when my shit is in the street."

"What do *you* think of this?" Coach asks my brother.

"Sole surviving son," Cody says. "Doubles the inheritance pool for me."

"Glad you're not *my* brother," Coach says, and turns back to me. "I can't promise you much playing time, buddy. Most of these seniors have three years' experience." He looks me over again. "And you have to admit, you're not exactly . . . What do you weigh now?"

"One thirty."

He stares. Cody looks away and smiles.

"Okay, one twenty-three. Listen Coach, I'm not the delinquent ant crawling up the elephant's leg with sexual pleasures in mind. I've always had a fantasy of playing ball. I could turn out to be a weapon on special teams or something."

Coach palms the back of his neck. "Well, I've never turned a kid away and I'm not going to start now. As long as you know what you're getting into." He stands. "You get this squared away with Coach Gildehaus today."

If Coach knew what I was already into, he wouldn't give this a second thought. Football's tough but it doesn't usually kill you. He's right about my being a cross-country stud, which is a bit of a miracle itself, given my revolutions per minute are double those skinny long-legged dudes I run against. But I'm a guy who does what it takes and if I can do what it takes in cross-country at this height, I can do what it takes in football at this weight.

Sure there are guys out there twice my size, just like there are guys in cross-country with twice my inseam, but the only reason I never turned out before was fear of permanent damage, and permanent won't last as long now. And shoot, even Jim Brown couldn't have taken a straight shot from a hundred-twenty-three pound bowling ball, if it was rolling fast enough. Sports is about concentration and confidence. There were about five million high school roundballers who could run faster, jump higher, dribble behind their backs and between their legs better than Larry Bird, but not one of them could hang on the court with him for the time it takes a bull rider to get points, even *now*, and he's been retired forever. It's in the mind. Plus, I'm blessed with one thing no one on our team or any other team has. I'm blessed with nothing to lose.

Three

"You're going through with it," Marla Dawson says, eyeing the cleats protruding through the open zipper of my workout bag.

I drop the bag next to the chair across from her desk and sit. "I'm like a genuine gridiron hero."

She smiles. "Only smaller."

"Only smaller."

"You're going to have to help me with this," she says, studying my face. "It's incomprehensible to me that you want to spend your last . . . this time, being pummeled."

"I just need something that grips my attention tighter than reality," I say. "Man, you see those big guys coming, it takes everything you have not to burrow into the grass like a gopher."

Marla Dawson is Doc's and my compromise. He was *this* close—forefinger and thumb maybe a quarter inch apart—to breaking confidentiality and calling my parents. "There will be a day," he said, "when I look back wondering what I should have done. I've got to live with myself." There was an implied *And you don't,* so we agreed I'd talk with a shrink at least twice a week and he'd find a way to fund it. Of Trout's 943 citizens, not one of them is a shrink, or even plays one on TV. I figured I'd bring that to his attention after he got a little more comfortable with reality. Only Doc Wagner is not so dumb as I'd like to think, because he happened to know our county is included in an outreach program out of Ada County, which means Boise, and that we have us a traveling shrink. Guess how often.

Marla's laugh at my gopher remark is tentative. "I'm out of my depth here," she says for about the eighth time in the four weeks we've been meeting. "I've worked with suicidal kids and kids who have lost parents and siblings, and even one kid who was terminal, but I've never worked with someone who doesn't care he's dying."

"So you'll want me on your resume. I'll sign anything."

"I want you on someone else's resume," she says. "You make me crazy."

"I want *that* on *my* resume." Driving a therapist crazy is like scaring a NASCAR driver with a Kia.

Marla can't be more than ten years older than I am. She's been a psychiatric social worker maybe three years, total. You don't draw Trout, Idaho, duty if you're Sigmund Freud. "You can write your doctoral thesis on me when I'm gone."

She's wrong, of course. Just because it feels *congruent* in some unexplainable way doesn't mean I don't care or that I'm not scared. I've begun jerking awake in the middle of the night, sweating in the wake of unremembered dreams, getting up to touch my stuff–running shoes and CDs, my leather jacket, my beaded Indian belt–sitting on the end of my bed in the dark trying to wrap my imagination around the fact that in a relatively short time I will simply be gone. But with my fear comes intense curiosity. It's hard to imagine what *isn't*. I rethink and rethink and rethink and rethink my decision not to tell my brother and my parents, not because I've begun to believe I could tolerate how they would treat me after hearing the news, but because I worry about how betrayed they might feel that I didn't let them prepare. The thing that bothers me more than my dad's bewilderment, and whatever effect this shit will have on Mom, is my brother's rage. When I go down for the count and

Cody finds out how long I knew, he will be one pissed quarterback.

"So how are you otherwise?" Marla says, bringing me back into her office with a *swoosh*. "And don't say 'I'm dying' again. That was barely funny once."

The more I tell Marla Dawson how I am the more she doesn't get it, but I have to admit it feels good to say it somewhere I know it won't get out. This isn't a story about some pathetic kid who goes terminal and freaks out before learning to live with the certainty of death and squares up all accounts on his deathbed only to have his brother make a million dollars later selling the story to Lifetime. I may be only eighteen, but I've been around long enough to know that some accounts don't get squared. This is a story about a kid who always knew at some core level he was moving on early and, even through the initial terror and disbelief, is going to figure out, come hell or high water (I vote high water), a way to consolidate a life into a year. Before Doc told me, I thought I had time to play, but now this year is my life. I have maybe twelve months to fall in love, marry, make smart investments, grow old, and die. But it's relative, right? There are insects that pack it all into a day. I was going to do maintenance work on my GPA while reading every book I could get my hands on that would teach me about *real* life, run my heart out in cross-country, make a few extra bucks from the Hall brothers washing and waxing cars in their showroom at Trout Auto when they needed it, and see if I could muster the guts to spend some of that money on Dallas Suzuki, who's tall enough to slow dance with her chin on my head (and my head in a sweet, softer place), to do just that. I've traded in the running for football, increased my reading time exponentially, and . . . well, Dallas Suzuki, brace yourself.

According to the laws of probability as outlined in Bill Bryson's *A Short History of Nearly Everything* (which, if you want to know what the universe is *really* about, you will read), I won the lottery to the power of about three hundred just being here. You too. Even if you start counting possibilities after the earth got formed, which the odds were way against, one botched life of a direct ancestor, going all the way back past salamanders, and your number doesn't pop up. Also, according to Bryson, if you packed the entire history of the earth into one day, life in its most basic form would start around four in the morning, you'd get maybe twenty minutes of dinosaurs around ten thirty at night, and humans would take up about the last minute and seventeen seconds.

So if you look at the difference between your life expectancy and mine, which relative to those numbers is so infinitesimal it could be represented by Sooner Cowans's chemistry grade; and you figure how much of your life you're going to waste because you don't know when it ends and how much of mine I'm gonna fill up because I do, we got dealt about the same hand which, if you think about it, isn't exactly an ace-high straight flush.

"I'm good," I tell Marla, in answer to her question. "I figure if Doc is right about the time I have left, I should wrap up my adolescence in the next few days, get into my early productive stages about the third week of school, go through my midlife crisis during Martin Luther King Jr's birthday, redouble my efforts at productivity and think about my legacy, say, Easter, and start cashing in my 401(k)s a couple weeks before Memorial Day. I don't have to worry about making enough money to put kids through college so I can focus on the more philosophical elements of my life." I unzip my backpack and haul out my notebook. "I have it charted here if you want to see."

"I think I've got it," she says. "So where do I fit in?"

"Problem solving," I tell her. "And convincing Doc I'm not crazy for refusing treatment."

"And how do you propose I do that? He calls me twice a week asking if you've changed your mind."

"Favorable psychological assessments," I tell her. "He needs to know he's done everything he can, which he has. I mean, he could have stopped me from playing football."

She nods. "He's sticking his neck out for you. And the problem solving?"

"Well, if I'm going to put the lid on adolescence in the next few days, I pretty much need to get laid."

Marla blanches.

"Not with *you*," I say. "Dallas Suzuki."

"What's a Dallas Suzuki?"

"Only the focus of my lust and my undying love."

"In that order?"

"You should see her."

"I have to say it offends my feminine sensibilities to help fuel the rocket of your sexual intentions, young man."

"But you need to remember that as your rapidly expiring client, *I* set the agenda. And besides, if you knew Dallas Suzuki you'd worry about protecting *me*."

"How do we go about this?"

"Methinks we need to make me more virile," I say.

Marla looks me over with the identical expression

Coach Banks flashed when I told him why I was turning out for football.

"Use your imagination," I tell her.

"I'll try."

"We might not have the horses in any given year to take it all the way," Coach says between earsplitting whistles in the middle of infinite wind sprints, "but ours will never tire down the stretch." That's horse-racing talk for the fourth quarter. Coach bases our capacity for pain on what he calls the principle of cardio bulimia. Simply put, that means we stop running when the third guy chucks up. It's a good skill to perfect if you happen to be a frosh or sophomore struggling to get into the good graces of the starters. In fact we select a "Player of the Day" in the locker room after the second practice each day and that award always goes to puker number three, who also gets divine dispensation from the wetted end of Sooner Cowans's towel. This football team is in killer shape, and if we run into teams with more talent, that's what will pull us through.

"You were *hittin'* out there today." Cody throws his gear into the back of my 1941 Chevy pickup.

I began coveting this vehicle when I saw it in

Coach's backyard three years ago. I couldn't believe it still ran. "Kissed my first girl in this sweet ride," he told me then. "If you promise to do the same I'll give you a good price." I said how about if I promised to kiss my *next* girl in it and he said that was good enough. It's Trout lore that the girl Coach kissed died in an awful car accident when they were seniors and he kind of spun out. He went to college to become an English teacher, taught in a few small towns in eastern Washington, then came home to bring closure to his interrupted life. I wonder if that closure ever came; he's been here twenty years, lives alone. I treat his pickup like a place of worship.

"Never underestimate the power of a midget on a mission," I tell Cody.

He hops into the passenger seat, snaps the seat belt low and tight across his lap, and smiles once again at the makeshift sign posted on the dash in front of him. SHOULD THE CABIN LOSE PRESSURE, AN OXYGEN MASK WILL APPEAR FROM ABOVE. BE SURE TO HELP THE DRIVER WITH HIS MASK BEFORE SECURING YOUR OWN.

"Just don't get your brain crushed," he says. "I need you."

The Creator of the Universe must have a sense of humor, giving the three-quarter-size Wolf kid perfect vision for diagnosing defenses and the Greek-godlike Wolf kid a brain that scrambles them on sight. Last year when he took over at QB, Cody and I stayed up late with the scouting tapes on the eve of every game. I'd teach him to read each situation and point out how one or two of the opposing players telegraphed their defense. Every team has someone to key on and I'm a genius at detecting them. This way Cody doesn't have to see the big picture. He says the college of his choice will have to cough up two scholarships, one for his body and one for my brain.

I start the pickup. "To crush my brain they'd have to find it," I tell him. "It's my spine that Sooner's shooting for."

"You do dreams?" I'm in Marla's office after practice the next day. School starts tomorrow.

"I took a class or two," she says. "I wouldn't exactly call myself Carl Jung. Why, are you having dreams?"

I take a deep breath. "You gotta promise not to tell. Who's Carl Jung?"

"The dream guru," she says. "And I'm a therapist. I *can't* tell. If I could you'd be the first one I'd tell *on*. Every member of your family would know what's going on and you'd be balder than a newborn on chemo and radiation and whatever else they do to slow this thing.

Ben, you're eighteen years old. I can't believe you're refusing treatment. Where is the disbelief? Where is the anger? Where is the magical thinking; the release?"

"I read that same book," I say. "I went directly to release. Those other phases end up in the same place, and I'm short on time. And I'll tell you something else. You'd keep yourself in work right up to retirement if you told my mother."

"But Ben, listen to me—"

"No, you listen to *me*. Do whatever you have to do to make it so I don't have to take care of you while I die. All my life I've been the kid who cuts his finger off and won't come in the house because he doesn't want to bleed on the rug, and if I'm going to do this year right, I gotta have somebody who thinks blood on the rug is decor."

She sighs big and looks off to the side.

"You'll have to do better than *that*," I tell her. "Let me see if I can make it easier. I am scared, but not exactly like I'm supposed to be. When Doc said I was dying, it was like . . . I don't know . . . *right*. I can't explain that, but it's just true. So yeah, I'm scared, *big*-time, but in the same way I knew it was right, I know something's next. I don't know what, but *something*. Did you know energy never dies? You can't kill it. And besides, I'm a hundred-twenty-three pound *kamikaze* on special teams. I'll get killed doing that way before some disease gets me."

She laughs. Tears rim her eyes, but she laughs.

I say, "Good. Now, do you do dreams?"

Marla rolls her eyes. "Why not."

"You'll want these in your thesis."

"And they are about . . . "

"They are conversations with Hey-Soos, which I recall word for word when I wake up."

"Spelled . . . "

"H-e-y-s-o-o-s."

"You're aware that H-e-y-s-o-o-s in Spanish is spelled J-e-s-u-s."

"I am aware of that, but I'm pretty sure he spells it this way. I mean, he didn't say that, but in the dream I know it."

Marla flips open an imaginary notebook and touches the tip of an imaginary pencil to her tongue. "And how long have you been hearing these voices?" She really is going to be good at this some day.

"Paranoid schizophrenia," I say, "a diagnosis you can live with."

She folds her hands on the desk. "So, real conversations with Jesus-spelled-H-e-y-s-o-o-s?"

"Yeah, well, you know, real in the dream."

"Does Hey-Soos tell you you're out of your mind playing football?"

"As a matter of fact, he does."

"What does Hey-Soos look like?"

"Like he should be pronouncing his name the other way. You know, sandals, bathrobe; got that hippie thing going. Dark, could be Mid-Eastern or Latino. Definitely a guy who gets harassed by Homeland Security."

"Are you messing with me?"

"I do," I say, "but I'm not."

"So what do you and . . . Hey-Soos . . . talk about?"

"This is the part you're going to think is crazy."

"You're way late for that."

"We talk about what to do with my life."

She nods. "And does Hey-Soos say what that might be?"

"This isn't your run-of-the-mill savior," I say. "He plays his cards close to the robe; makes me come to my own conclusions."

Marla shakes her head and sighs. "Well, I guess I should welcome the help."

Four

"Little Wolf, how are you doing this?" Coach has called me into his office after practice. This place is a trip through Trout athletic history. There's a framed picture on the wall of Coach and Boomer, Sooner's dad. Man, one look at that guy and you know why Sooner doesn't have siblings. This guy eats his young. That year's quarterback stands between them, for which Coach looks plenty happy. The Idaho state championship trophy for the two-mile run sits on a table just below that picture, then there are a few years missing, followed by paraphernalia highlighting some event in football or track for each year Coach has been back. To the untrained eye it might look like the storeroom in the back of a sporting goods store, but my eyes trace these walls with reverence. Nobody I know loves what he does more than Coach Lou Banks.

"How am I doing what?"

He sweeps his hand, palm down, in front of the window looking out into the locker room. "*This*," he says. "Football. You're flattening guys half again your size."

"Focus," I tell him. I give him my theory on Jim Brown in the path of the rapidly accelerating one-hundred-twenty-three-pound bowling ball. "Why?"

"I want to learn to coach it," he says. "No offense, but you're not exactly in possession of an NCAA Division One body, for *any* sport. Coach Gildy and I used to sit around after your cross-country meets and laugh our asses off at your turnover rate. Man, you must have worn out some shoes."

That's pretty funny. "It's all math," I tell him. "The shorter the stride, the faster the drumbeat."

"And how the hell are you getting to all these tackles? I've clocked your wind sprints and you might be the sixth or seventh fastest guy on the team. Yet you're in on almost every damn tackle."

"I'm tellin' you, Coach: *math*. You gauge the speed of the guy you're after and chart the angle quick enough to know where he's going before he does, then give him the big surprise. A football field is finite on all sides; the mathematician conquers the speedster almost every time."

Coach palms his neck. "How do I put that in the language of the average football player?" he says.

"The average football player doesn't speak a language," I say back. "And you might notice something else. I may be the sixth or seventh fastest wind sprinter at the beginning, but clock me toward the end."

Coach looks wistful. "I played like you once, maybe not as smart, but as hard. It's good to have you, Ben. Plus, you keep your brother levelheaded." He's quiet a moment. "Listen, buddy, these first weeks you're looking tough enough to start. . . . "

"But like you said, you got guys who've been busting their butts for three years, waiting for that starting spot. Give it to 'em. Most times I won't be the difference between a win and a loss. When I am, put me in. Otherwise, I'm fine with special teams." I don't want to sound like some kind of saint or something, but if this disease takes me out in midseason and they're counting on me, it could be hard to fix. And no way do I want anyone hating me for taking his spot. I probably won't be around long enough to fix that. It's good to drum up a little contempt for the guy running ahead of you on the cross-country team because you both get to run anyway, but you don't want disharmony with your buds on the gridiron.

Coach pops me on top of the head. "You're a good man. How's the ol' pickup running?"

"Runnin' good," I tell him. "And I'm getting ready to christen her."

"Feel free to keep it to yourself when you do," he says.

I said before, Coach has long felt like a second dad to me. Coming on to Christmas of Cody's and my eighth-grade year, the world was right. Mom was on her meds, we had three feet of snow, it was clear and cloudless and "colder 'n a well digger's butt in the Klondike," as Dad put it, casting the valley and mountains in heart-stopping postcard beauty. A great hunting season augmented Dad's mail and freight business, and Cody and I brought in extra money of our own shoveling sidewalks and pushing cars out of ditches; you couldn't have crammed one more present under our tree.

Then around December twentieth Mom flushed her medication down the toilet and on the twenty-fourth downed close to a fifth of Jim Beam whiskey and turned Christmas Eve into Halloween. The crazy chemical unbalance she achieved would have sent Freddy Krueger running for cover. My mother's shrill, rageful voice echoed through the neighborhood as Coach pulled up to let Cody and me out after caroling up at the county hospital, and through the window we saw the living room filled with smoke. Coach ran inside to find Dad pinning Mom to the couch and a smoking, water-soaked pile of ashes beneath the tree. Dad had got to her as the fire started up the tree and kept us off the next night's evening news. Coach took Cody and me to his place. We didn't get any presents that year, but we skied and snow-mobiled all Christmas Day with Coach before settling down in his tiny dining room for one of the worst turkey dinners I have had the pleasure of choking down. Since then he's been our go-to guy when the shit-storm starts.

Coach probably could have gone anywhere and done anything he wanted, but he came back home. Trout High School stands on the same ground it stood on when he went here more than twenty-five years ago, though it's been remodeled. Hidden on the south side of the building, there's a tree with a plaque set in concrete near the trunk. It says, IN MEMORY OF BECKY SANDERS. Everyone knows Becky was Coach's girlfriend. She died in that awful accident at the river bridge south of town.

Coach had been the scourge of the school that year after he stomped off the football field when his racist coach had ordered an illegal hit on a black player from another school—the only black player in the league—and Sooner's dad did the dirty deed. That ended Coach's football career. By his own account he wasn't a particularly talented football player so he turned himself, on guts alone, into a better small-college distance runner than his talent should have allowed. Football was his first love, after Becky, and I think he came back here to get the bad taste out of his mouth from that last year. And he stayed. Now that I know I'm on my way out, I'm worried that he likes me so much, with a dead girlfriend in his history.

If we win it this year it will be because of my brother. Physically, he's got it all. We run a single wing, which is, like, pre-Pleistocene and never seen in eleven- man, but it's perfect for a quarterback who's as good a runner as he is a passer and that's my brother. Even with his dyslexic defensive reading skills he's almost impossible to corner because of his speed and quick release. He's upchuck scared before every game, dead sure the other team will figure out he's fooling the world, but the second the kickoff whistle blows he transforms into a football machine. God, I love to watch him play.

• • •

One thing about attending a high school with fewer than a hundred students is you're offered one teacher for each subject and if you don't get along with him or her, suck it up. It's worse with a required course because, well, it's required. I'm pretty sure teachers sit in the teachers' lounge with the same lament about us, but at least they're getting paid.

First period of the first day of school I realize if I'm going to maximize my education this year, I'd better take control. Mr. Lambeer, our U.S. government/current events teacher, underlines that idea for me in spades. As a junior I took U.S. history from him, and dutifully wrote down everything he said, regurgitated it on tests, and walked away with an A. Since then, however, I've begun reading *Lies My Teacher Told Me*, by James W. Loewen, which tells how the twelve most popular high school history texts are way more interested in making us love our country and revere all the famous historical dudes than they are in getting the facts right. As near as I can tell, Lambeer told every lie in the book, and added some whoppers of his own. So I'm figuring what's true for history, may also be true for government.

"You may as well all know I'm conservative and

proud of it," he says. "Damn proud of it, in fact." I don't doubt him; he looks plenty proud. "Best you know where your information is coming from," he goes on, "and though I'm conservative, I'm also open-minded to others' ideas. So feel free to disagree with any political thing I say. But be ready to defend your position, and I'll warn you I was considered a pretty darned good debater in college."

Lambeer's hard to take; wears a suede jacket with those leather patches on the elbows, khakis, a sweater vest, and brown loafers. The man is dapper; and though he says he welcomes political debate, he's known to get pretty surly when he doesn't bring you around to his position, which should make him fun to mess with.

We sit in traditional rows in his room and he loves to walk up and down the aisles with a rubber-tipped pointer as he lectures or asks questions. Lambeer is the guy who, by his very existence, taught me the meaning of *pontificate.*

"We'll cover the structure and meaning of the Constitution in a matter of weeks," he says, "so we can put it in today's context. I'm interested in relevance." He goes on to make clear what a miraculous document our Constitution is, how it has stood the test of time with relatively few changes—amendments—over its more than two hundred years in existence.

"Did you know the Framers recommended we revisit the Constitution about every twenty years?" I ask.

"Excuse me?"

"Yeah, they knew things change, that the Constitution could get stale in the face of progress."

Lambeer takes a deep breath. "We'll get to questions and discussions later, Mr. Wolf." He turns back to his notes. "The Bill of Rights—the first ten amendments to our Constitution—is the perfect example of laws that stand up in any age." He raises his eyebrows at me.

I raise my hand at him.

"Mr. Wolf, I said—"

"I know, but what about the right to bear arms?"

"What about it?"

"Do you think the Framers of the Constitution knew that amendment would put semiautomatic weapons in the hands of teenagers like my brother, intent on blowing away their classmates?"

Cody points a cocked finger at me.

Sooner Cowans says, "Jesus, Wolf. Right to bear arms just means everyone can have a gun."

Lambeer ignores him. Sooner's not exactly the guy

you want on your side when trying to make an intellectual point. "Do you believe the second amendment to be a bad one, Mr. Wolf?"

"It was meant to arm a well-regulated militia," I say. "I think it needs to be more exclusive."

"If we take away one person's right to own a certain gun," he says, "where does it end?"

"Have you read *Outgunned*, by Brown and Abel?" I ask. This reading binge is turning me into a force to be dealt with.

"That's a liberally biased piece of . . . That book has an agenda," he says. "It's an outright attack on the National Rifle Association."

I start to answer but he says, "Hold that thought; we'll come back to this."

"Let's back up one amendment," I say. "Do you subscribe to the concept of separation of church and state?" I say *subscribe to.* Whew. I might have to get leather patches on the elbows of *my* jacket. First I'd have to get a jacket.

"Yes, I do, but I also know that our nation was founded by Christians as a Christian nation, so that concept bears qualification."

"Actually the fact that we were founded by mostly Christians is probably a reason to make *sure* we enforce that separation," I say. "That keeps laws fair if we, like, try to *hedge* to the Christian side of things."

"Mr. Wolf, what have you been reading?"

"Just a bunch of subversive stuff," I say.

Dallas Suzuki says, "Remind me to get his reading list."

I am speechless. I'd walk proud and erect through gunfire for Dallas Suzuki's *grocery* list.

"We'll postpone this discussion until we can get through this early material," Lambeer says. Back to his notes. "In addition to the Bill of Rights–"

I say, "Did you know that 'under God' wasn't part of the Pledge of Allegiance until the early nineteen fifties?"

"MR. WOLF!"

It is clear I have begun my quest for truth in Constitutional education with a little too much zeal, so I zip it for the rest of the period, in order to finish it in class instead of in the office.

First game of the year, against Meadows Valley, Cody is *en fuego.* Sooner Cowans, the aforementioned Son of Kong, runs the opening kickoff back to their ten, broken loose by a bullet block from Trout's own hundred-twenty-three-pound helmet with legs, and Cody fires a perfect rollout pass to Andy Evans on a down-and-out to the corner of the end zone. We're ahead by one touchdown with twenty seconds gone in the first quarter and that's as close as Meadows gets. Cody throws for three more, Sooner runs for two, and our sophomores play nearly the entire fourth quarter. I play on all special teams, which in this case is mostly our kickoffs and their punts, so I'm in on about one play in four. By mid-second quarter I have a little cult following of Impossible Dreamers in the stands and I'm thinking this change of career direction was a great idea. Even *their* coach comes over after the game to ask what spaceship I rode down on. Coach Banks says again he doesn't know how he's going to keep me out of the starting lineup on defense, but I tell him again to keep me a surprise. Truth is, the less other teams see me, the tougher it will be to figure me out.

My first words *ever* to Dallas Suzuki: "Bad news. Conventional jock wisdom says you girls will have to wait." My diagnosis has turned me into a much more forward dude.

Dallas looks up from the open econ book next to her food tray to where I would be towering over her, had I the power to tower. She doesn't miss a beat. "Wait for what?"

"Us," I say. "Jocks. Studs."

"What are we supposed to wait for you jocks, studs, to *do*?"

"That thing we do."

"Hatch?" She goes back to her book.

That didn't go exactly as I planned it, so I invite myself to sit across from her. She reads on.

"Have you thought about your future?"

She releases an exasperated sigh, closes the book. "Have you thought about yours?" It's stated as a threat.

I have thought about my future plenty because I can think of it all in one thought, but saying that is not going to get Ms. Suzuki into my pickup. "I have," I tell her, "and I see you in it."

"As a friend or a pugilist?"

"Actually, I hadn't thought it out that far," I said, "nor did I know I had a choice."

"Tell you what," she says, opening the book again. "Let me finish this now, and meet me around seven thirty tonight at The Chief. We'll discuss this long wait I'm in for."

I walk away from *that* conversation way further ahead of the game than I *dreamed*. Let me be sure you understand the level of my good fortune here. Dallas Suzuki is like the best mix you could get of Japanese and Caucasian. She's tall—listed 5'11" in the volleyball program—and you can't even tell if she's beautiful because she doesn't look like any girl you've ever seen. I've attended every Trout High volleyball game for the past two years just to see her legs. Her muscular thighs and calves give her hops so major she blocks out the sun if you're on the other side of the net, and the width of her shoulders makes her appear to be dangling from a wire hanger. There's not one part of Dallas Suzuki's face or body that is in any way Miss World, but you put it all together and I'd swim through five hundred yards of molten turds to listen to her fart into a paper sack over the telephone.

I pirouette out of first lunch.

"I know who you are."
"Who am I?"

"You're me. My therapist is a dream lady. She brought me up to speed on your act. Everything in a dream is part of the dreamer."

He smiles beatifically, sips wine from what looks like an ancient goblet. "I'm you in ways you can't even imagine."

"But that messes me up," I tell him. "That's not the kind of thing I would say, or even think. And where'd you get that thing you're drinking out of? How can you be me if you say and do things I don't know about?"

"I don't know," he says. "You're the one who said I was you."

"Yeah, but you agreed. You said you were me in ways I can't imagine."

"Two very different things."

"So how's this work? Can I, like, ask you questions? Like any questions?"

"Any questions," he says.

"And you'll answer them."

"If I know the answers."

"Well, if you're not me, then you have to be like a spirit or a ghost or something. So you should have answers," I say.

"Who made you an expert on spirits and ghosts?" he asks. "Look, don't worry about it; I'm here to help."

"Did Jonah really live inside a whale for a while?"

"It says 'big fish,' not 'whale.'"

"Okay, did Jonah live inside a big fish?"

"Not even a worm lives long inside a big fish. Next question."

"Did Adam and Eve really live in the Garden of Eden?"

"Why're you gettin' all biblical on me?" he says. "And why the history quiz?"

"I'm trying to figure out who you are, really, 'cause in case you didn't know, I'm dying and if you're even related to who I think you are, that's a hell of a resource. I mean, Hey-Soos, that's like Spanish Jesus. I could get wise beyond my years real quick. Think of the spread I could get in the yearbook."

"I'm not related to who you think I am, any more than you are, at least."

"But you know Him, right?"

"Do I know Jesus? Who doesn't know Jesus? Or about him at least. You sure you want to spend your last days getting into a high school yearbook?"

"Maybe not as a major goal, but it wouldn't be a bad fringe benefit."

"You're worried about how you're going to be remembered." It isn't a question.

"Yeah. I guess I am. You think that's bad?"

"It is what it is," he says. "You wouldn't be the first. But you worry about your legacy and you'll spend all your time trying to create something you have no control over. It's all in good works, my man. It's about influence, about what people do in your name after you're gone."

"Were you a real guy once? Is that how you know this?"

"I thought you said I was you."

"Okay, okay, I don't know. Maybe you are and maybe you aren't."

Hey-Soos nods.

"Well, were you?"

"I'm not here to talk about me," he says. "I'm here to talk about you. You have so much to do with so little time, as they say."

"Now, see, that could be me. That's kind of what I've been thinking. So you could be me. Hey, I know. What's two hundred forty-three thousand divided by a hundred and seven?"

"How would you know if my answer is correct? I didn't see you bring a calculator into this dream. Ben, you have a little less than a year. How much of it do you want to spend testing me?"

He's right.

A distant, loud "William Tell Overture" causes Hey-Soos to shove 'er in reverse and back into the darkness. I push the snooze button on my cell phone alarm in hopes I can get in a couple more questions, but he's out of here.

Five

Just because Coach Banks wants his football team to be one with the student body doesn't mean certain individual players feel that same Zenlike love. With its 943 citizens and its student body count of ninety-three, Trout is Odessa, Texas, Lite. If you don't get the reference, read *Friday Night Lights*. Read *Friday Night Lights*, anyway; it's hella good. Then watch the movie. Anyway, suffice it to know there are guys in this town who remember the 1965 state eight-man championship as the greatest day of their lives. Boomer Cowans played on the 1982 championship team (the same team from which Coach Banks made his premature exit), and every player on our team but one crosses the street when we see Mr. Cowans coming, to avoid a rundown on his annually inflated statistics along with a graphic description of what a wuss our coach is. Mr. Cowans stayed in Trout after high school in an attempt to clear-cut the trees from every mountain within two days' drive. He and his compatriots logged themselves out of a job and now he works for the county as a heavy machinery mechanic and advises each new generation of Trout Cougars on the best illegal ways to separate an opposing player from his spleen. His son, Sooner, the one guy who *doesn't* cross the street when he sees him coming, does not exactly adhere to Coach Banks's vision of "One School, One Team." He doesn't even see the other football players as part of his team most of the time. This isn't a case of the apple not falling far from the tree; the apple didn't fall. He won't mess with my brother because Cody's the guy who does or doesn't hand him the ball, but anyone else is fair game. Sooner operates below Coach Banks's radar most of the time but if you don't have at least three tattoos of dragons or sharp objects or motorcycle shit, you don't want to get caught alone in the men's can with him. He's fast and he's fearless—been whacked by his daddy harder than any football player in the league could hit him—and even though I have nothing to lose in the long run, he's the one guy I cringe before hitting. His thighs are made of steel strands and he runs high knee, so if you don't hit him just right he'll realign your skeleton. Because he's our kick return specialist and I play special teams, I get him full speed every practice. But every shot I get, I take. The ugliest sound in my life is his laugh when those that I take bounce off him.

My brother throws his duffel bag into the back of the Grey Ghost, which is what Coach christened his pickup before it was mine, and hops in shotgun. "Take me home, little big bro. We'll get something to eat and go over this week's defenses. The *scouting* team was killing me today."

I was playing on the scouting team, the team that plays the next opponents' defense against the first string, and watched my brother's eyes as he looked at one wrong cue after another. "There are two guys to watch on their defense," I tell him, "and you had your eyes on the other six, ten times out of ten. You'd better get your broken field running down if you're going to play it that way."

"We'll go over it tonight," he says.

"Okay, but late," I say back. "Say, ten."

Before I can tell him I'm spending quality time with

Dallas Suzuki I catch a glimpse of the shadowy form I know is Rudy McCoy sliding through a doorway in the alley behind Trout Auto and I hit the brakes. I put it in neutral, snatch a package from the jockey box, and tell my brother to take the pickup on home. "I'll be there in a half hour."

"What the hell are you doing?"

"Nothing. Just do as you're told." I laugh and punch his arm. The joke is that I'm the little older brother who always tells him what to do.

I step out as he slides into the driver's seat and the pickup roars away.

Once in the alley, I knock lightly on the side door to the garage. No answer. I walk around front and peer in through the plate glass windows. Rudy moves through the dark of the repair shop behind the showroom. I rap on the glass; he stops. I can't see if he's looking at me, but I point toward myself and make a half circle, signaling I'm going around to the side, which I do. I knock. Again. Louder. Nothing.

I pound.

"Whaddaya want?"

"In," I say.

"Whaffore?"

"Lemme in and I'll tell you. It's Ben Wolf."

"Who?"

"Ben Wolf. You know, the car wash kid."

"So whaddaya want?"

"In!"

The door opens and I step just outside the dimly lit garage. A single bulb burns in a small room off to the right. Rudy's room.

"You gonna invite me in?" I ask.

"Hell no, I'm not gonna invite you in. What do you want? What're you doin' here? You ain't washin' cars this late in the day." His voice carries its familiar alcohol-soaked slur. Rudy cleans up after hours. I don't see him much when I work, but he's lived in this little room since I can remember. We've said hello a time or two, but he always slinks away. No one talks with him much because he keeps a vampire's hours, cleaning and performing light maintenance while the rest of Trout sleeps. When he does come out in the light of day, he moves around town like a ghost. People walk past him without noticing. He asks again what I'm doing here.

"I brought supplements."

He stares, swaying almost imperceptibly. "Supplements," he says.

"Supplements," I say again.

"To what?"

"Your dinner. You been lookin' peaked lately, Rudy. All pale and shit. Here." I extend the paper sack toward him. "I separated 'em into little plastic bags. Take all the pills in one bag every day, right about when you eat. You'll feel better."

"I feel fine. And 'all pale an' shit' is how I'm supposed to look."

"Just try it," I tell him.

"Get outta here." He says it with little force. "I'm supposed to be like this. I'm the town drunk."

There's something about this guy. He does his job around Trout Auto and he doesn't have a family so he's not hurting anyone staying semiembalmed. But "I'm supposed to be like this. I'm the town drunk" is funny actually, and on the few occasions I've heard him talk before, that's kind of standard. Since Hey-Soos asked me what I wanted to do with this time, I've decided a little time with the least of my brethren might look good on my celestial resume and Rudy sure qualifies there.

"Look, you're a good kid . . . *maybe* you're a good kid," Rudy says, "so leave your minipharmacy on the bench and go home to your momma."

I set my individually wrapped nutrition Baggies out on the workbench. "One a day," I tell him again, and head out. Got to plant the seed.

"An' if you wanna keep bringing nutrients," he says as I reach for the doorknob, "bring something to wash 'em down with."

Dad says The Chief looks exactly the way it did more than twenty years ago when he was in high school: counter the length of one side, booths down the other, tables in the middle. There's a back room for banquets and wedding receptions. The six-foot profile of an Indian chief's head outlined in neon flickers just above the entrance, matching colors with the neon window sign that reads, EATS. Doesn't even say FOOD.

EATS. The lights shine bright in the near-empty room, and on the jukebox Emmylou Harris sings "Sweet Dreams" low and scratchy and not quite like Patsy Cline did before her. The Chief brags on having one of the last 45-rpm-record jukeboxes in the country. I live in *hick* city.

Dallas Suzuki sits in the far back booth dressed in jeans and a sleeveless blue-and-white Adidas shirt, scribbling furiously in a notebook. I stand near the entrance, watching—fantasizing about—her to my quickening heartbeat.

"What do you want?" Winona's voice whispers in my ear. "Besides her." Winona has been the waitress here long enough that she bought half ownership with tip money.

"Nothing. I want nothing besides her."

"I put an aphrodisiac in her water," she says. "Little guys get horny, too."

"Little guys get horny *especially*," I say back.

"Go sit. Got hot apple pie and ice cream coming."

I cross the tile floor to Dallas's booth, nodding to Mr. and Mrs. Morgan, who eat here every night. Sooner Cowans sits alone at the counter, eating a burger. Our eyes meet in the mirror and he quickly looks back down at his plate. I think I see a slight swelling on the side of his face. I say, "Hey, Sooner," but he doesn't answer and I don't push it.

I stand by Dallas's booth. "Hey."

"Hey," she says back, scribbling a few more words and closing her notebook.

"I didn't think you'd come."

Her face scrunches.

"Like maybe you forgot, or weren't serious."

"You thought I'd make a date at lunchtime and then forget by seven o'clock? What kind of girls do you go out with?"

I'm hoping tall multicultural ones with fetishes for diminutive dudes. I sit then nod toward the notebook. "So what's up?"

"I'm doing a personality profile for *The Coug.*" *The Coug* is our school newspaper.

"Anybody I know?"

"Our student body numbers ninety-three, Ben," she says. "What do you think?"

"Anybody I hate, then?"

"Not unless you're filled with self-contempt," she says.

Dallas Suzuki is doing a personality profile in the school newspaper about *me*. I'm instantly gratified, and disappointed. I was hoping she met me tonight for reasons considerably more torrid than a personality profile. Dare to dream. "What about my personality are you going to profile?"

"The part that drives a hundred-twenty . . . -thirty . . . How much do you weigh?"

"One seventy-five–"

"Maybe in lead pants," she says. "How much do you weigh?"

"I wasn't finished. One seventy-five, give or take fifty-two pounds."

"I'll take. The part that drives a hundred-twenty-three pound human to put on a football helmet."

"Illusions of grandeur," I say. I try to read her notebook upside down, hoping her diary is there, but all I see is a description of what I was wearing when I walked into The Chief. It says I'm cute. Funny, put this face on a stud hoss like my brother and he's ruggedly handsome. On me it's cute. *But* it says I'm cute.

"*Ill*usions or *de*lusions?"

"Focus on "grandeur.""

"Ah." She writes. "Coach Gildehaus said you were pretty much a lock for State in cross-country this year."

"I guess. He seemed cool with me switching. Said a guy's gotta reach as high as he can. I still feel a little bit bad about leaving the team high and dry, but half of those guys are in my new mini-fan club."

"I know. I interviewed a couple of them. They said they wished they had the *huevos* to do what you're doing. So," she says. "With your imminent success as a runner, what made you decide to turn out for football?"

Dying makes you want to tell as much truth as you can as much of the time as you can. There might be something at the gates to the next place requiring that. "I used to run pass patterns for my brother until it was too dark to see, then I'd watch him do his thing on the field and I ached to play a heroic sport like that instead of one where you're used as filler in the back of the school newspaper," I say with uncharacteristic candor.

"So you turned out for football because you were jealous of your brother." She scribbles. "You're going to take some heat for this."

"If you print it like that I will."

"It's what you said."

"I said I ached to be a hero."

"When you watched your brother. How about I say you used to run by the field on your sixth or seventh training mile and look at all those bruisers grunting and sweating and trash-talking each other and you picked up your pace and said, 'Those guys don't know what pain *is.*' So you turned out for football to show them."

"That could get me hurt . . . but I like it."

"Done." She stares at her notebook, then, "What's it like running around out there in the land of the giants?"

"What do you mean?"

"You guys have game tapes, right? You must've seen yourself on the field with those monsters. Even the little guys look big next to you. You look like a special effect."

"Hey, I was on the school paper last year. What kind of journalism is this?"

"What about Ben Wolf the student?" she says.

"The student?"

"Well, you're not just some mindless superstud, right?"

"You're right, not *just.* I'm attending some classes."

"Which you have to do in order to play football," Dallas says. "What's next for you?"

That's a question I'm not prepared to answer, so while I don't tell *the* truth, I tell *a* truth. "I'm going against the 'senioritis' grain," I tell her. "This is going to sound sick and wrong, but now that you've come to know and love me I know you'll soften it for publication. I'm going for it all this year. We're headed out into the world and in case you haven't noticed, they're not preparing us."

Dallas puts her pen down. "You want to go off the record on this?"

I stare at her notebook. "Yeah, probably I do."

"Okay," she says, "go on."

"No teachers better be tryin' to slip anything past me, because I'm a be lookin' for truth." I open my backpack and dig out my copy of *Lies My Teacher Told Me*. "Did you know Woodrow Wilson was a white supremacist? They have schools named after this guy. All Lambeer ever told us was that he tried to get us into the League of Nations." I flip some pages. "Did you know Christopher Columbus was a huge catalyst behind slave trading all over the world? Lambeer talks about him like he's Jesus's brother or something. It's like people don't think teenagers think about real life, like we're all about sports and parties and *Rock 'n' Roll High School*. No real synapses fire until the magical, and arbitrary, age of twenty-one."

"Add Japanese concentration camps to that," Dallas says. I happen to know she's one of those students who has taken her education seriously from day one. A suspicious kind of person might think that's the reason I'm dropping this on her, but they would be only partially right.

"Yeah, no shit. Japanese concentration camps. Good old World War Two."

"Well, I'll leave all this for another story, maybe one I write after final grades are turned in."

"I appreciate it."

She picks up her pen and notebook again. "Do you have a date for homecoming?"

"You're putting my romantic status into this?"

"God no," she says, slamming the notebook shut. "I'm asking you to homecoming."

I'm going to need therapy after this.

Six

"That *threw me for a loop.*"

"*I heard your heart beating all the way here when she asked you to homecoming.*"

"*I thought I recovered nicely.*"

"*Perspective is important.*"

"*Everything's relative, right?*"

Hey-Soos smiles. "*Never forget that.*"

"*Man, I gotta tell you, when I got to spend one second with her, I hated that I'm short-term. I kid around about her, but, I mean, did you see her? Did you listen to her? Feel what happened inside me? Of course you did, you're me, or you're Hey-Soos, or . . . Man, if I weren't dying, you'd be freaking me out. I mean . . . never mind. Sheesh. I wish I'd known a long time ago she'd talk to me. Look at the time I*" *wasted. What am I going to do about this?"*

"I vote you go to homecoming with her."

"Go to homecoming with her? Go to homecoming with her? Of course I'll go to homecoming with her. This is like getting your dying wish. It is my dying wish."

Hey-Soos says, "You're speaking in tongues."

"You seem rattled today," Marla Dawson says after my third or fourth attempt to describe Dallas Suzuki's allure.

"Chart that," I tell her. "This could be, like, a breakthrough." That's what Marla calls it when I say something worth writing down. She charts it. So far she hasn't charted much.

"You think you're pretty funny," she says, "but you are truly rattled. I may not be Sigmund Freud, but you would be well advised to talk about things like this in some detail."

Marla is right. It's hard for me to talk about anything here without joking. She's said before that when I get so close to telling real truth I use comedy as a shield. Hey, when you're walking around a high school so small everyone not only knows everyone else but might be related, and your *younger* brother, who looks exactly like you only life-size, is the school's superstud, *and* when you're dying, comedy is what you have. Don't get me wrong; I love it that Cody's a superstud. I just don't always like the comparisons.

But Marla wants serious, and I should give her serious. She's *not* Freud, but she's plenty smart. New, and scared, but smart. I know I have to get to the serious side soon, because shortly I'll be living on borrowed time. I try to return to the feelings I had sitting in The Chief with Dallas, because they *were* serious. I close my eyes and picture her. "Did you ever have a feeling that you were *connected* to somebody? I mean the minute you see them, or have some stupid little conversation where neither one of you said anything important, but . . . " I open my eyes and see tears welling in hers. "You have," I say.

She clears her throat. "I have."

"Who . . . "

She reaches for a Kleenex. It's like I kicked her in the gut. "Keep talking. I'll save this for *my* therapist."

"Therapists have therapists? Whoa. And I'll bet those therapists have therapists, too. I'm looking at infinity." She looks wounded and I back way up. "Sorry."

She says, "You felt a connection."

"Yeah. I mean, I've had my eye on Dallas Suzuki since she moved here, but she's . . . you know, she could have maybe not *any* guy but a whole bunch of them who are . . . I don't know."

"Don't sell yourself short," Marla says.

"I can't sell myself tall."

Her eyes roll. "What does it take to keep you focused?"

"An answer to this dilemma?"

"You have to stay focused so I know what the dilemma *is*," she says. "Stay on *task*."

I rise a few inches and sit back down hard. "On task. I looked across that table, and Dallas was finishing up with some meaningless statistics about my life for her 'profile,' but she had already asked me to homecoming and I couldn't even hear. I just kept thinking of the night. You know, of the dance. Coach always picks the toughest league game of the year for homecoming, and it will be over and we'll have won it and I'll be all dressed up and she'll be . . . oh, man . . . "

"How do you know you'll win?"

"Because I'm going to homecoming with Dallas Suzuki and I will not allow it to be on a loss. Anyway, have you ever been with someone and even though you haven't been there before it just seemed . . . "

"Like something inside you was touching something inside her?"

Whoa again. "That's exactly what it felt like. Dallas is, like, one of the toughest, smartest kids in our school, girl or boy, and she was being her same tough self. But there was this feeling, like I knew her. That part had nothing to do with my loins, which were also stirring. At any rate I started feeling this . . . this *grief.*"

Marla nods. "Which makes sense."

"How does it make sense? I just got to talk to her for the first time right then, and she asked me to *homecoming.* I should be happier than a pig in shit."

"But like you said before . . . "

I sit back. "Yeah. I swear, sometimes I forget. I'm gonna feel bad any time I get anything good, 'cause I have to give it up."

"You have to feel that way unless you do like you said," she says.

"Right. A day at a time."

"You told me to hold you to that. I'm holding you to it."

And that's the way I'll do it. A day at a time. An hour

if need be. A minute. Like I do football; one hit at a time. You think a guy my size could hit Sooner Cowans like I do if I thought about having to do it again?

"I heard three guys talking about the Horseshoe Bend game today," Coach says. We're huddled around him in the end zone near the end of practice. "That's an extra six wind sprints." His whistle pierces the crisp air and we line up. As usual we run until the third guy chucks up something special, and then know there are six more. Coach runs those last three beside us, hollering. "We don't play Horseshoe Bend this week! We don't play Horseshoe Bend this week! Who do we play this week?"

A couple of guys grunt out, "Council!"

"Can't hear you," Coach hollers. "You owe me *suicides* at the end of these! Who do we play this week?"

"COUNCIL!"

We're back at the starting line, the six extra wind sprints history. *Suicides* are normally a basketball drill. At the sound of the whistle, you sprint from the baseline to the first free throw line and back, then to the half-court line and back, then to the far free throw line and back, then to the far baseline and back. That's one suicide. On a football field, it's to the twenty-five and back, then the fifty, then the seventy-five, then a hundred. And *back*.

In the end zone, Coach is the only one standing. "Guys, if we look ahead, somebody's gonna come along and ambush us, sure as hell. Talent-wise we should be able to spot Council a couple of touchdowns, but they run back one kickoff or a punt or hop on a fumble at the wrong time, then stuff us on defense and that's wiped out. There's a reason the preseason pick to win the college national championship usually doesn't even make it to the game. They forget to see somebody coming who wants it worse than they do. Now, one more time. Who do we play this week?"

"COUNCIL!"

We beat Council 28–7.

Sooner stalks the frosh and sophomores with a snapping towel in the locker room afterward, and even though they all got playing time, this is the most dangerous part of their day. Sooner's towel is a poisonous snake's tongue. Coach will halt it in a minute if he sees it, but Sooner is sneaky and like I said, Coach's "We Are The World" attitude isn't exactly his life philosophy. Sooner feels negligent any time he walks out of a room and someone smaller than him isn't crying.

My brother catches the tip of the towel on the back-swing and jerks it out of Sooner's hand. Sooner whirls, ready to swing. "Nice game, Cowans," my brother says. "Took two or three a' them there Lumberjacks to pull you down ever time. Whaddaya think you were gettin' a carry?" Sooner doesn't recognize my brother's spot-on imitation of him.

Sooner forgets he was about to raise a three-inch welt on some third-stringer's baby butt. "Had one eighty-three," he says. "You gimme the ball fourteen times. What is that?"

"A hair over thirteen," my brother says. "*Damn,* man! MVP numbers." He looks at the side of Sooner's face, at the same bruise I saw in The Chief. "Looks like somebody popped you, man."

Sooner touches his face. "Fuck you, Wolf."

Cody smiles. "Man, you got bad taste."

Sooner smiles. So does the kid who just avoided losing a piece of his ass. That's Cody. Smooth.

"Let's get something to eat and you can start me on the Horseshoe Bend videos," Cody says as he throws his gear in back of the pickup after we shower.

"It's Friday night," I say. "You get something to eat and Dallas and I will get something to eat. There's a dance at the Legion Hall. You can have your choice of cheerleaders or girl jocks except for one, and we'll do the videos tomorrow."

"What happened to 'Keep it in your pants until the end of the season'?"

"C'mon, Coach said that's just an expression *his* coach used. He meant stay focused. And I am focused. And you will be too as soon as I get you going on those videos. Horseshoe Bend is *meat*."

When we get to the house, the front and back doors are open and we hear the vacuum and old-time rock 'n' roll spilling out of the open windows. Mom is on a tear. Dad's truck is gone, which means he's been here and is probably warning the folks at Emergency to be ready. Cody grabs my shoulder as I start inside. "Let me take care of it," he says. "If you go in there, you'll be there all night and Dallas will miss her shot at the greatest pint-sized lover of all time."

I start toward the door anyway and Cody wraps me up from behind, playfully, but he isn't letting go. "You can't fix this, little bro. Every time you try and every time you fail. She'll either wear herself out and come down or she'll go to the hospital and come down. But your lifeguard act has no effect. We'll do the tapes tomorrow like you said. I'll catch up with you at the dance." I hate to admit it, but as much as I have the eagle eye on the field, Cody has it off. Mom's big swings don't affect him like they do me. I feel her swings in my bones. Every high, every crash.

A *crash* is what Dad calls what happens when Mom comes to the end of a *run*. He calls her manic stage a *run*. When the crash starts she tries to keep the run going with alcohol, which is a way bad idea because alcohol is a depressant even though it feels initially like it's giving you a boost. When I was little I'd want to go outside and play with my friends or see a movie and Mom would be in the kitchen, drinking whiskey and Diet Coke from a glass hidden in the cupboard, washing dishes or cleaning up, ready to tank. It started with a sigh, just as I got to the door.

"What's wrong?" I'd say.

"Nothing." But the tone of "nothing" meant "everything," and I'd feel an ache. I'd think if I'd let her talk for a minute she'd feel better. She'd say she was a bad mom and I'd spend fifteen minutes arguing, numbering all the good things she did for us, but that just gave her ammunition to deny it. The more she denied, the more desperate I'd get and we'd be there for hours; Cody would leave and come back when his game of hide-and-seek or kick the can was done and all our friends were in their houses. Mom would wear out and I'd go to my room, believing I had saved her. Within days the bedroom door would close and Cody and Dad and I would eat our dinners at The Chief and Doc Wagner would come over and get Mom on meds and she'd start to float back up.

I always believed if I'd said the right thing, made a *little* more convincing argument for her motherhood, I could keep her afloat. Dad went unaware for years about those conversations because they happened while he slept on the couch in front of the TV. He probably saved my emotional life the night he overheard, waited until Mom went to bed, and explained her condition to me. "You can't convince her because she needs to crash. *What* she talked about means nothing; she talks so she can crash."

It's funny. The front door to our house is huge double French doors that open onto our lawn from a sunroom just off the living room. The back door is a tiny door in the kitchen leading to a cluttered porch you can barely get through for all the shit Cody and I leave there. I could have walked out that front door and totally avoided Mom, but until my dad explained things to me, I never once used it. And I never once made it through the kitchen.

At the dance I get a little taste of the football hero thing and if I'd known it felt this good, I'd have turned out a long time ago. It would be worth it to go through life crippled to feel this good, even if you were going to have a long one. The cheerleaders meet me at the door and hoist me onto their shoulders. I'm the only guy on the team who gets that kind of treatment because, hey, cheerleaders have a load limit. Dallas stands back, watching and laughing, relaxed because their first volleyball game is a week away. My guess is she'll be more focused when that happens. She's a monster on the court, and word is it takes her a while to come down.

About ten thirty Sooner promises Jack Badley, the band guy spinning the CDs, weeks of crippling pain if Jack doesn't let him take over the mike for a while, and when Sooner plays a slow one so "you studs can git you some," Coach Gildy threatens to feed Sooner the mike. Fortunately the Legionnaires only let us have dances down here if we can provide a chaperone, and Gildy is usually up for that. Gildy's built slight, like a runner, but he is made of titanium. The guy can do, I shit you not, two hundred fifty push-ups without stopping. Sooner gives up the mike.

"Can't you guys keep him under control?" Gildy says as he approaches Dallas and me standing by the door.

"Hey, Coach Gildy. Yeah, you'd think he'd listen to etiquette tips from the likes of me."

"Not really," Coach says back. "You'd have to tell him what etiquette means. Hey, you were spectacular out there today. You've been out for the wrong sport all these years."

"Maybe," I say. "Still feelin' a little bad for jumping ship on cross-country."

"Don't do that. Life's short. Do what you love."

"You want to come in? No one's home."

I'm guessing my surprise is showing. "Inside your house? I thought . . . " I catch myself.

"It's a *rumor* that no one ever comes inside my house."

It may be a rumor, but it's one nobody disputes. It's understood that Dallas doesn't bring people home; not even girlfriends or volleyball team members. It's so well known it doesn't even seem weird anymore. "How many other kids from school have been inside your house?"

She smiles. "Well, if I get you and snag one more, that'll be two."

"That's what I thought."

She holds the door open, eyebrows raised.

"You sure it's okay?"

"I said, nobody's home."

"Would it be okay if they were?"

"I'm the one who doesn't bring people here," she says. "Mom doesn't care. And Joe Henry has friends over all the time."

"So where are they?"

"Boise," she says. "Mom had to take him to the dentist, and Joe Henry doesn't go to the dentist without getting to stay overnight in a 'fancy hotel.' They won't be back till tomorrow. He stays in a place with a swimming pool or we pay dearly."

I do a quick recap. I'm coming off one of the best all-around days of my life: we kicked the Council Lumberjacks' asses into the hills, I've been dancing and talking and being cool with a girl who could own me with a frighteningly low bid, it's half past midnight and that girl is inviting me into her empty house. I have no idea what she has in mind because everything about her so far, starting with her giving me a second look, has caught me off-guard. I don't have a curfew because my romantic history is such that my parents never thought I needed one. Submit this story to an editor and it's returned as too much fantasy even for fantasy.

"Sure," I say. "I can come in for a little while."

Now I don't kiss and tell and I think only dickwads brag about their sexual conquests, but I'm dying and this is my first and final story and I have to say it like it is. We get to the part in the *Friday Night Lights* DVD where the cheerleader takes the quarterback into the bathroom to make him prove he's not gay, and all of a sudden we're up in Dallas's bedroom and I'm proving I'm not gay.

"Whoa! What was that?" I'm lying in Dallas Suzuki's bed with her and I am out of my element and I probably don't have to tell you what an understatement that is.

"That was sex," Dallas says, and rolls over facing away. I'm thinking I don't want to be one of those guys who scores and leaves, like they talk about in every *Men Are Pigs* HBO comedy special, so I'm already thinking of excuses on the outside chance my mother is still up and running, keeping Dad awake. I don't have a curfew, but they do expect me home *some*time. A flat tire won't do it; you can walk from one end of Trout to the other in about thirty minutes. Even if you're coming from the old graveyard it's about an hour. Two stud athletes like me and Dallas could make it in forty minutes. Can't say one of my relatives died; Mom and Dad *are* my relatives. I'm working on a really stupid story about having had to drive Dallas to Boise because of some emergency her mother had. . . .

"You'd better get your stuff and go," she says.

"What?"

"Get your stuff and go."

"I'm not one of those guys who–"

She rolls over and smiles. "I'm one of those girls who," she says and tweaks me on my cheek. "Go home or you're gonna get in trouble."

I'm sitting on the end of the bed pulling on my shoes. "I'm not sure what I'm supposed to think."

"You're supposed to think you just had a really nice time," she says.

DUH! "I'd like it if I was supposed to think that *you* just had a really nice time, too."

"You should think that, too."

"Yeah, but what beyond that?"

"Don't go there." She sits up, holding the sheet high with one hand and cupping my chin in the other. "Hey, Little Wolf," she says. "We're cool, okay? Now go home before your parents send the cops. It's after two."

I sit at the lake in my pickup, staring at the half-moon reflecting off the water. I want to close my eyes and dream up Hey-Soos, but that requires getting the other part of me out of the way and so far, I can only do that in near-dream state, and that requires bed. My mind skips like a flat rock sailed onto the glass-smooth surface of that lake. I can't tell if I'm closer to Dallas or further away. I wanted more response; wanted her to want me to stay. But if we *are* closer, then what? I mean, I'm like the worst kind of army brat or something, here for the year and then gone. Only I'm really gone.

Seven

"I've spent as much time as I'm going to on the basic structure of our government," Lambeer says. "We've covered the material well in spite of Mr. Wolf's attempted blockades, and your book serves as a solid reference. I expect you to know that structure when you address an issue. Clear?" When Lambeer says, "Clear?" it isn't really a question. He's telling you it is.

"Fifty percent of your grade will come from your civics project," he says, "so those of you who haven't, best be selecting one. Again, you can choose from the handout I gave you on the first day, or you can conjure up your own, though of course it will be subject to my judgment." He stops beside my desk. "What is this you're reading, Mr. Wolf?" He touches my paperback with his pointer.

"The Autobiography of Malcolm X," I tell him.

"Interesting taste," he says. "Have you something against Dr. King?"

"Nope," I say, "but Malcolm was a pretty interesting guy. Came up the hard way."

"Indeed. He had some radical ideas, don't you think? A little far from the mainstream."

"I'm not done with the book yet, but yeah, I'd say he was a little out of the mainstream."

"Far enough out to get him gunned down by his own people," Lambeer says.

Cody says, "Aw, man, you ruined the ending for him."

Lambeer taps my head with the pointer. "You have a clever brother. I suspect you already knew the ending. By the way, you're one of the few who hasn't chosen your project. Can you have it by the end of the week?"

"That I can, sir."

In the cafeteria Cody and I sit at a table alone, going over this week's defenses. Dallas drops her tray next to Cody. "Oh, you big tough football boys, teach me the basics of your game. How come all the guys who play football have such big shoulders?"

"Those aren't real," Cody says. "We wear shoulder pads. Hey, Dallas."

Dallas plops onto the bench in front of her tray, runs her fork through the Spanish rice, and wrinkles her nose. Her bare foot sneaks up under my pant leg. "You been racking your brain for someplace nice to take me soon, Little Wolf? We do want to keep this 'thing' going, right?"

"I was thinking about taking in a volleyball game," I say back. "Nothing else to do. Wanna come?"

"I mean, *after* the volleyball game. And you'd *better* be thinking of taking in a volleyball game unless you want your pitiful little life to get more pitiful." Dallas is pretty vocal with her feelings about the differences between emphasis on boys' as opposed to girls' sports.

"Only fooling, dear," I say. "Only fooling."

Trout's opening volleyball game against Salmon River is a barn burner. The sort of Asian-looking girl with the leap that blocks out the sun is everybody's MVP. On her talent and guts alone, Trout takes it to a fifth, tie-breaking set. Dallas Suzuki is everywhere, diving for balls only extreme sports dudes try for and drilling kills

Sooner would be afraid to block, but in the end, it's a team game and she doesn't have much of a supporting cast this year.

In the Grey Ghost afterward, she is inconsolable. "You had a great game," I say, touching her shoulder.

"We lost."

"Yeah, but Jesus . . . "

"We lost."

This will not be a warm and fuzzy night. After one bite of her burger at The Chief, she tells me to take her home. "Nothing personal," she says. "I'm just a bad sport."

When I drop her off she doesn't want me to walk her to the door, which means she doesn't want me to kiss her, so I peck her on the cheek and watch her stride across the lawn, and I am overwhelmed with that one thought that sneaks up and whacks me across the back of the head when I least expect it. Enjoy it, buddy. You're dying. A block from her house I pull to the curb and let the fear crawl into my throat and almost strangle me.

"What you doin' up this time a' night?" Rudy sits by the workbench, looking way better than I expected.

"I might ask you the same thing," I say.

"I'm a vampire. What are you doin' here?"

"Didn't want to go home," I tell him. "Thought you could use some company."

"You're running around in the middle of the night and you decide the town drunk needs company? I think not."

"It's true."

"Well, you're wrong." Then, "What's in your back pocket?" he asks. "Lemme see that."

I take out *The Autobiography of Malcolm X,* which loosens my pants. It's a big damn book, even in paperback.

"Serious literchur," he says.

"You know Malcolm?"

He holds the book, staring at the cover, turns it over in his rough hands. "Oh yeah, I know Malcolm," he says, and disappears for a moment into his room. He comes back with his own copy, opens it, and shows me Alex Haley's autograph. He holds the book like a Bible. "Malcolm used to get my juices goin'," he says.

I nod toward his room. "You have other books in there? You read books because you're alone so much?"

He gazes across the room at the workbench. "You thought all I do is drink?"

"I didn't mean that."

"Being alone isn't new. No worse than my years as a priest."

Whack! "What?"

"What," he says back.

"You're a priest?"

"That slipped out. Forget I said it."

"A Catholic priest?"

"I said, forget–"

"Too late."

"Ex-priest. And keep it to yourself."

"Shit, who'd believe me?"

"I mean it, you tell no one." His voice has completely lost its slur, turned to a dialect I couldn't distinguish from either of my parents'. It is deep and resonant. I can't help but look at him funny.

"It's a long story," he says.

"Tell me."

"No chance."

We stand, staring at each other. "Okay, then," I say finally, "I won't tell anybody, but you have to tell me more about Malcolm X."

"That could be arranged, but not tonight."

"Thanks for letting me . . . you know, stop by."

He nods, touches my shoulder. "Go."

Now *that* has to be one of the top five strangest things that's happened this year, which is saying something when you consider a doctor told me I'm dying and Dallas Suzuki asked me to homecoming and took me to heaven and then sent me on my way, *and* I'm starting special teams on a *football* team. First he's Rudy McCoy the town drunk, then he's Rudy McCoy who sounds like he stopped drinking, then he's Rudy McCoy with an *autographed* copy of *Malcolm X*–which, I shit you not, is an *amazing* book–and then he's Rudy McCoy the ex-Catholic priest. I think when you're dying you start looking for important things in the corners. You can't let anything that seems even semi-important pass, because it passes forever. Things take on *meaning*. In my pickup on the way home, I'm figuring Rudy McCoy is somebody I'd better get to know better.

The Horseshoe Bend game is fast approaching and all of Trout is holding its breath. I'm up till the wee hours with Cody every night, playing and replaying the HB tapes Coach Banks gave us, studying the physical nuances of the two or three players who don't get that they're telegraphing Horseshoe Bend's every intention. We've got tapes from all their games so far, thanks to the compulsive nature of Gustavius O'Brien, who needs an A in phys ed to keep aloft his four-point-plus grade point average and who can't dribble a basketball twice without sending it scooting off his foot and under the bleachers. He convinced Coach it's as valuable to record physical activity as it is to perform it. Coach wasn't hard to convince: Gustavius provides some primo game tapes.

Horseshoe Bend's center linebacker—also their QB—a monster Basque kid named Johnny Bilbao, who probably averages fifteen tackles a game, leans back ever so slightly on his haunches when he's expecting a pass and also lilts slightly to the side he thinks a running play is going. His predictions are uncanny, but Cody's quicksilver when it comes to improvising on the run, and if he catches Bilbao leaning the wrong way for a micro minisecond after the hike, he can burn him at least once out of ten times. It could come down to that with Horseshoe Bend. They've got studs at the same positions we've got studs, so gaining a fraction of an advantage on one out of ten plays could be the difference. Cody and I refuse to lose this game; that's all there is to it. We watch Bilbao three hours straight. He's smart as a whip; he'll figure out Cody figuring him out.

They've also got Elston Thomas, a linebacker, and Matt Miller, a defensive guard, who could make Sooner's day a long one. They're both about his same size, and though he's faster, Sooner tends to think he can run right over anyone who gets in his way, and these guys are way tough. Miller takes out the interference and Thomas cleans up after him. They can switch sides depending on the running tendencies of the other team, so it'll be impossible to run away from them. You see them lining up, time after time, against the oppositions' strengths. But we counter with Dolven and Glover, who consider it a personal affront each and every time either Sooner or my brother is touched by an opposing player behind the line of scrimmage, and they're pretty quick and versatile, too; and Andy Evans, a threat to catch almost any short ball Cody throws, who doubles as a defensive safety and claims *no*body gets behind him. He's right more often than not.

This is going to be a good game.

"You and Coach are going to have to call *smart* to keep these guys off balance," I tell Cody. "And you might have to call more audibles at the line, which is not your best thing."

"Wish you were on the field with me," he says.

When we played backyard ball as kids, Cody and I were always on the same team and he'd check the call with me. Sometimes he just let me make it.

"If I'm not on the field with you in high school, I'm sure as hell not going to be there in college," I say. "We'll go back through all this as soon as we're sure you have these tendencies down. You tell me what you'd call in any given situation and I'll tell you if we're in synch." Actually most of the time we are on the same page, which would be Coach's page, too. A given play in a given situation usually just makes sense. It's those few times when you can call against the grain that you give yourself a little edge. That usually happens on the field.

After several more hours about 95 percent of our play-calling is identical. "Let's get some sleep," I tell him. "You gotta be rested come Friday. Boise State scouts."

"We'll tell 'em we're a team," Cody says.

"We'll tell 'em shit," I say back. "We want them looking only at you. They don't give scholarships to guys who come with miniature look-alikes."

"You're right. We'll unveil you when we get there."

"Right."

* * *

In bed I drift; feel myself slipping toward a conversation with Hey-soos, but I want it too bad, and when I want it too bad Hey-soos makes me wait. I breathe, like Hey-soos taught me, and repeat my mantra: *Little Wolf, Little Wolf, Little Wolf.* It's what I imagine the fans chanting. Not exactly Buddhist.

"Hey, Little Wolf."

"Hey, Hey-soos."

"Getting complicated, huh?"

"Does the Pope wear a beanie? Is Sooner prehistoric?"

"Not really, but I get the point."

"Yeah, we're probably all the same in your eyes."

"Maybe not all the same, but I stand in a place that gives me a broader perspective. What's up?"

"If you stand in a place that gives you a broader perspective, you should know."

"Man, why you busting my chops?"

"You're right. You think we have a chance against Horseshoe Bend?"

"I know who I picked in the office pool."

"But you won't tell me."

"Life's no fun without risk," he says.

"I'm worried about my brother."

"But you know your brother is going to be fine."

"He was counting on me next year. I mean, no college coach is going to let me have anything to do with their football team, but Cody leans on me. Just having me around . . . "

"But you know your brother is going to be fine," he says again.

"Yeah."

"So whassup?"

"You know Rudy McCoy?"

"I know everyone you know."

"Do you know people I don't know?"

"Stop wasting your time trying to figure out who I am. Rudy McCoy."

"He's important, isn't he?"

"Does he seem important?"

"I mean, to me."

"Does he seem important to you?"

"Did you know people on this planet get paid up to a hundred fifty bucks an hour to do what you're doing?"

"What's that?"

"Ask questions and never give answers. They're called therapists. I have one."

"So why are you talking to me? Wow. A hundred fifty? Am I good? At least I'll know what to come back as. You were talking about Rudy McCoy."

It's hard to figure how to get answers out of Hey-Soos. He never says something is or isn't going to happen, and he won't tell you whether something is the right or wrong thing to do. That exasperates me cubed, but when I get past trying to wrangle answers out of him, he usually brings me around to finding my own. He's like a good math teacher. But I'm like a bad math student: I want the answer and I don't want to show my work. I'm dying and I'm impatient.

He says, "There's time for everything, Ben."

God, it's like he hears me thinking as well as he hears me dreaming. This is so *bizarre. "I'm trying to figure out what to do about Rudy McCoy. I get it that he's important if he feels important, but I don't know what to do."*

"Want some advice?"

"Jesus, I'd pay for advice."

"It's Hey-Soos," he says. "And it wouldn't help. I'm on an expense account you wouldn't believe. Here's your advice. Pay attention. Use your mind. Use your instincts. You'll know what to do. Not just with Rudy McCoy, with everyone."

● ● ●

Coach stands at the door to the locker room before our next practice. "Sooner is out."

That plays to a stunned silence.

"Broken collarbone," Coach says.

My brother says, "What happened? I saw him after practice yesterday and he was fine." Sooner wasn't in school today but there wasn't even a rumor.

Coach's head tics slightly to the side and he doesn't answer. "This changes things for Horseshoe Bend," he says. "More option plays, Cody. You have to be at the top of your running game as well as your throwing game."

Cody nods. He's already rethinking. Suddenly we have hours' more tape to watch. Cody *has* to feel prepared. Cody has to feel overprepared. The option calls are easier to go over because the choice to throw or run, or the choice to pitch or run, happens after the action starts and that's Cody's strength.

"That also puts big pressure on our defense," Coach says. "Ben, I'm bringing you in at safety. Andy, you're coming up to fill Sooner's linebacker spot." Andy Evans winces and nods. We've just given away eighty pounds on defense.

● ● ●

Thursday morning Sooner walks into class with a thick cast evident under his shirt and his forearm held tight to his chest with a strap.

"Hey, Sooner," Randy Dolven says. "Whassup?"

"Fuck you."

"Sooner," Glover says, "what happened, man?"

"Fuck you."

Cody points at him. "Hey, Sooner, man. Me too?"

"You too," Sooner says. That's the sum total of what we hear about Sooner's broken collarbone.

Eight

Fridays aren't heavy days for jocks at the learning factory. If it's a home game, which homecoming obviously is, we're dismissed just after noon to dress down and get taped so we can get a good warm-up and pummel those posers into the Stone Age. If you think there's a chance any one of us is going to concentrate on quadratic equations or what Coach thinks Charles Dickens meant or any current event other than the college football rankings, you are exceedingly wrong-minded. Before first period we're all on the lawn passing a ball, soaking up the adulation of the masses.

Because it's homecoming not just the players get out early. Picture Neil Armstrong returning from his walk on the moon, scale it down to a Trout-sized town, and you have the visual. The band will be on the field an hour before game time entertaining the spectators. The pep club will be on the field selling hot dogs and Pronto Pups and pop and candy. The Horseshoe Bend spectators will double our population.

And then, Sooner or no Sooner, we'll kick their asses. Like I said before, we won't have it any other way.

The football field is three miles out of town so we dress in the locker room and ride the bus.

Sooner comes up behind Cody and me, places his good hand on Cody's shoulder pads and says, "Sorry, man. It's fuckin' killin' me not to be out there today."

"Me too," Cody says. "But we'll get it. We'll get it for you."

"I dunno if you can get it without me," Sooner says, and I feel Cody stiffen. You get a fleeting sense that Sooner doesn't want us to win this because of what it will mean about him.

Cody punches his good arm softly. "It'd be a lock if you were there, but we'll do what we have to do." That's my bro. Doesn't leave anyone hurting except players on the other team. It's hard for Sooner to hear. Having people do things for him isn't exactly how his life has worked out so far. He nods, still staring out the window. "My fuckin' ol' man did this."

Cody says, "Aw, man. What happened?"

"Got drunk like always," Sooner says. "Started raggin' on me 'cause he thinks you get all the press when I'm the workhorse. Calls me that. Workhorse. Fuck. One good thing about my ol' man: he makes me look smart. Don't know what I was thinkin', but I tol' him we was both good and . . . aw, shit. Who cares?"

"So why'd he break your collarbone?"

"'Cause he was drunk, ya dumb shit. Jesus, didn't you hear me?"

Cody doesn't take the bait. "Yeah. I heard you. You're right. Dumb. Wasn't thinking. Hey, I'm sorry, man."

Sooner turns away. "Fuck it."

Cody and I look at each other, heads shaking in unison. He says, "I'll take a crazy mom over that any day."

If anyone else heard Sooner, they don't show it. Everyone's focused on these next three hours.

We pile off the bus next to the field and take a slow lap, just inside the track. The fans cheer and it's hard not to break into a run just to drain off some of the adrenaline.

Coach Banks and Coach Langford stand in one end

zone and we trot in for calisthenics. Cody leads them alone because Sooner is on the sideline.

Cody brings me with him when we line up in first-, second-, and third-string warm-up offenses, and I stand beside him listening to his running monologue as he reads the imaginary defenses, correcting him when he forgets something. It's like cramming for a test you've already crammed for, but there's no telling Cody that. I just hang close and answer on cue. We're whispering into each other's ear holes right up to the time he walks out for the coin toss. Sooner walks out in his street clothes for that, and I use the time to loosen up.

We lose the toss and will kick off. "Bilbao sits back on his haunches when he expects a pass," Cody says.

"Yeah, you can barely see it, but look at his cleats; that's how you tell."

"And when there's a blitz on . . . "

"Thomas taps the lineman on the hole he's going through, twice on the butt. Real subtle, but he does it every time. Then he taps the side of his helmet twice."

"He has to tell the other linebacker he's going in," Cody says, and slaps my shoulder pads. "If we win this, bro, I'm gonna buy you something big."

Now I concentrate on the kickoff. Horseshoe Bend is

big and they're fast and their coach isn't likely to go light on prep for special teams. I can tell by the way the big guys come at me these days, I'm not the surprise I once was, so I have to get smarter and smarter to stay on my feet and do my damage.

In the pregame huddle, Coach runs over assignments, identifies their studs by number one more time, and covers strategy for helping out when someone's overmatched. I've got nothing on my mind but the ball and getting my helmet on it.

Then we're on the line and the whistle blows and I am shooting down the outside about 95 percent, watching their return develop. We kicked away from Bilbao because he's run two back this year, so number 26 snags it and they're coming my way. I sidestep one block but get knocked over by the second and am up almost before my knee hits the ground. Cody is two steps in front of me and Bilbao has streaked across the field to lead their blocking. Their collision creates a sonic boom and both are laid out and I'm leaping over their pile, staring right through 26's face mask, and I go low, right at his thighs, wrap my arms around him, and hold on for dear life. Dolven drills him a second later and they're first down on the twenty.

This is the first time I've stayed on the field after a kick-off and the Ben Wolf mighty midget fan club goes wild.

Andy Evans is a good, smart athlete, not as talented as Sooner, but good enough to start on any other team in the league. He's not used to the linebacker spot, though, so I'm ready for extra business. Safety is exactly that, the last guy back, and my job is to make the tackle if the guys up front don't get it done, and to cover passes, of course.

Horseshoe Bend comes out running and throwing short, so Cody and Andy get most of the action and I just back them up and come in hard once I see the play develop. I'm relieved I can see just as well when I'm playing as when I'm watching. If Mom and Dad had put a little more beef into my conception, I'd be a danger-ous dude. I'm not getting any solo tackles, but I'm in on a lot; one sends electricity down my spine when I team up with Ron Coburn, our defensive end, to take Bilbao down. Hitting him is like hitting Sooner. You gotta make like you're not afraid to die.

Toward the end of the first half Cody slips around end on an option and slides in for a score. Coach calls an option pass and Cody runs in the point after. You don't get a lot of great kickers in high school football, particularly eight-man, so almost everyone goes for two. On Horseshoe Bend's next set of downs Bilbao eats up the field on three- and four-yard runs, they get forty on a pass 'cause I went with the wrong receiver, but I run their guy down at the twenty. Bilbao shoots up the middle on the next play leading interference for their other, unsung, halfback; Bilbao levels Cody and their guy drags me into the end zone. Bilbao blows their point after and we go into halftime up by two.

"I think we can throw more on these guys, Cody," Coach says in the end zone during the break. "You're running more on the option, but their defensive backs are getting tired and Evans is getting open." Andy nods. "Keep a lookout," Coach says. "We'd better sting these guys quick. They're not gonna lie down."

Cody nods and scoots over next to Andy, grilling him on who he thinks he can beat. Andy's got just okay speed, but he's crafty as they come and if he can get his hands on a ball, it sticks.

The worst part of homecoming is halftime. The band plays. The drill team marches. The cheerleaders dance. The homecoming queen gets crowned and rides around the field at no miles an hour and we sit in the end zone getting rigor mortis.

• • •

We receive to start the second half and Cody and Andy hook up on a couple of short ones before Cody fumbles the snap and they take over. They go three downs and punt and we do the same and that damned Bilbao brings it all the way back. He jukes the first tackler, then cuts back across field, away from me and Cody. Cody locks on him and he's gaining, but somebody puts a honey of a block on him and suddenly it's me and Bilbao and then it's just Bilbao. He was too far away for me to get an angle and they've got us 12-8 because they blow the point after again, which gives us a *little* window. We're back and forth in the middle of the field through the quarter, no one's scoring, there is earthquake-style hitting. If one side of my body isn't numb, the other side is. Both teams are clean and well coached and *no*body wants to lose. Even with teams in as good shape as we are, guys are wearing down, and I know it's my time.

I've worried all along that my disease would catch up with me, but it hasn't, and it won't start during the fourth quarter of the Horseshoe Bend game. I've run every wind sprint, every suicide drill, every play, as if it were my last. I'm making each second of my life count, and I'm spending anything I saved up, right here on this field, right here on this day. I've gone full bore on special teams and defense all afternoon and I feel fresher than I did at kickoff. I'm in pain every time I hit, but I cause pain every time I hit, so who cares. This season ends for me with no regrets. As Coach says, you can measure your love of the game by what you bring off the field with you. If you come off the field at the final gun with nothing, that's perfect love. It doesn't mean I can't make mistakes, but they'll never be because I'm tired and they'll never be because I'm not thinking. My mistakes will come from excess.

With four minutes left in the fourth quarter we're still playing down one touchdown between the twenties and it's starting to dawn on me that we may not pull this off. Cody and Bilbao are racking up yards and tackles (though I've gotta be leading them both in tackles) but neither can get the ball into the end zone.

Then we get the break we've been looking for. Horseshoe Bend tries to put it away with a long pass and Cody picks that baby off on our three-yard line and hauls ass. They bring him down on the fifty and we are *wired*. Cody fires a short one to Andy out in the flat and another to Dolven on the other side on a guard-eligible pass. He gets two more first downs running for short yardage on the options and we're on the twenty-seven with a little more than two minutes to go.

Coach signals for time and Cody calls it, trots over. I stand close so I can hear. I'd give *anything* to be on offense so I could be in there for the end of this game. Cody takes off his helmet. "Givin' 'em their money's worth today, huh, Coach?"

"You're givin' me a heart attack," Coach says back, and laughs. "Okay, all short stuff. Cautious but aggressive. Keep running those options. Do *not* throw into heavy coverage. We can take our time; don't want to leave them a lot of time after we score. Now let's get this." He slaps Cody on the butt and Cody runs back onto the field and completely fucks it up.

We flood the right side with receivers and Cody rolls out right and there is Andy Evans on the two and he has his man beat by at least two steps. Cody fires it *behind him.* Shit! And Johnny Bilbao comes out of *no*where and sticks Andy in the chest so hard his helmet pops off *as he reaches back.* The ball flies straight up and into the hands of number 23, whoever the hell *he* is, and he's got a clear ninety-nine-yard shot at our end zone. Cody recovers and runs him down on our thirty. Andy is still down looking like a purple-and-gold rock, and when they get him up he's got a one in seven chance of telling you what day it is. That's it for Andy Evans. We've got two minutes, Horseshoe Bend has the ball first and ten on our thirty, and our undefeated season seems *over*.

In the defensive huddle, my brother is calm as he was at the coin toss. "My fault, guys, but we've got time to get it back. They think they can get one first down and then run out the clock. Tackle the *ball*. Strip 'em. Get it loose any way you can. It's gonna be in Bilbao's hands, so it won't be easy."

Bilbao gains three on the ground on the first play and he's holding on to the ball like a Brink's driver with a ten-pound gold brick.

"I'm guessing run again," Cody says to me as we line up. "Let's give 'em a little safety surprise. I'll blitz and you come in right behind me; see if we can shake things up."

We get our break. Horseshoe Bend wants to shock us with a quick score and Bilbao goes back to pass. Cody opens the hole and I shoot through as Bilbao looks for his receiver. He's cocking his arm as I drill him in the solar plexus, and bounce off him like a bullet off Superman's chest, but I hear the air go out and seven guys hollering "Ball!," which means it's loose. It's not loose for long, though. It's under Dolven.

"Put my brother in," Cody says to Coach on the sideline.

"What?"

"He's been running pass patterns for me since we were in grade school. He can catch anything I throw. Andy's out. They'll think we threw Ben in to fill the hole."

Coach looks at me. "He's right," I say. "Anything he throws." What I'm *thinking* is, Anything he throws when there's not someone ready to take my head off the minute I catch it, but I only smile.

Coach says, "It's different in a game."

Cody looks down the bench. "See any Hall of Famers?"

As we near the offensive huddle Cody says, "Drop the first two."

"What?"

"We're seventy yards from the goal," he says. "If we nickel and dime it we'll run out of time. I'll get us one first down running, but I want you to look like these first two passes are the first you've ever seen. Run bad patterns. Look like you're trying to fake your guy out but don't get away from him. Let 'em know this isn't your position. They'll back off you and we'll burn 'em long."

I start to question but Cody says, "Do it." For this moment, he's the older brother.

In the huddle he calls my number without telling the team his plan.

Now I may be the guy with the eye for tendencies and the football brain in the bedroom, but Cody is the real deal when the action starts. Once he's on the field he's either the best athlete out there or he can make you think he is.

He fires to me on first down and it's all I can do to drop it. I block it with my body and let it bounce off my chest. Coach puts his hands in a T for time, but Cody shakes his head. He hands off to Glover, whose biggest claim to fame up till now is clearing out the hole for Sooner, and Glover picks up six. Cody options the next one and steps out of bounds just past the first down marker. A hair more than a minute on the clock. I'm coming off my position like a first-practice freshman and can already feel them cheating a bit; leaving me. My fuckin' brother is a genius.

Glover gets a yard on first down. On second and nine, Cody fires me another short easy one rolling to his right, and I drop it, too. Back in the huddle the guys stare at Cody like *I thought you said Sneezy has been catching your passes all his life,* but Cody glares back and nothing is said.

Cody gets another few yards running, but can't get out of bounds and the clock is ticking–time for one play. He slaps my ass and says, "Play Mr. Klutz for a second and then slant for the left corner." In the huddle he calls an option pass rolling out to the right, flooding the right side with so-called receivers.

Glover fakes a block and comes out of the backfield looking for the short pass; our tight end crosses from his spot and runs deeper to that same side; I let my guy knock me down, scramble up, and head for the opposite corner like somebody poured Tabasco sauce in my ass. And damned if Bilbao doesn't hold back and come after me from the other side. I've got about three steps on him, but he's a legitimate speedster and I'm an illegitimate speedster. He's five inches taller, and Cody's going to have to throw this back across the field, which means it has to go over Bilbao *just* enough for me to snag it. It's like throwing a football through a tire–a hundred yards away, with the wheel still in it.

And my brother does it. The ball sails a fucking microinch over Bilbao's outstretched hand, which is about half a fucking microinch above my head, and settles onto my fingers while my feet are still in the air on my belly flop into the end zone. ESPN for sure. And I am buried. The entire team is on my back and my face mask is imprinting the grass. I can barely breathe.

The band breaks into the Cougar fight song in the bleachers and every other Trout citizen storms the field. Andy was the only player hurt in the game, but there's a good chance more of us will join him if we don't get out of here. You haven't lived until you've had your helmet rattled by an out-of-work logger. We have given these folks a game to remember. Dad is pounding Cody's shoulder pads and ruffling my hair, yelling "Amazing! Amazing!" That's more emotion than you'd have gotten out of my father on the day either of us was born. Mom paces the sideline making sure everyone knows whose kids hooked up on that last play. Jeez. She's only known most of these people forty years; I guess they know who her kids are.

"You might just get to college on a scholarship of your own, little big bro," Cody says to me back in the shower. "Dang!"

I'm standing under the hot shower stream, my eyes closed, imagining the shower is in Dallas's house. It was a great game, but now I'm going to *homecoming*. With *Dallas Suzuki*. "You're ruining my concentration."

"Concentrate any harder and I'll have to cover you with a towel. Besides, you used all your concentration on that pass," he says.

"Didn't have to concentrate," I say back. "I'd have had to ball up my fists to miss that one. Boise State scouts got an eyeful today."

"Still only eight-man," he says.

"You could have thrown *that* pass to me alone in the desert," I say, "and they'd have signed you on the spot. Whoa!"

"I did put something sweet on it." He smiles.

"You boys played a marvelous game." My mother is standing in the kitchen fixing dinner and drinking whiskey and Coke out of a glass hidden in the food cupboard and mopping the floor and cleaning the corners of the small windowpanes looking out onto the front lawn. She is in full bloom. "I think you're both going to get football scholarships, I really do. And I think you should look at Notre Dame. Boise State? Boise State? My God, they'd have to give you full rides for yourselves and your children to justify your going there. You *have* to reconsider. They called, you know. They've already been on the phone to me. I told them we'd have to think about it. I said we'd just have to think about it. They should have been here with their offers at the beginning of the season. The price has gone up. The price has gone *up*. What a throw! What a catch! My God . . . "

Cody steps into the living room where Dad is reading the paper. "Hey, Dad."

"Hey, Cody."

"Tell me you got to the phone before she hung it up."

"Close, but no cigar," Dad says. "But I did call them back. You're covered."

"Thanks."

"Only here to serve," Dad says. Mom rants on from the kitchen. She thinks she's talking to me, but I'm in the doorway listening to Dad and Cody, wishing I could stop what's about to happen.

"She about to crash?" Cody asks.

Dad nods toward the kitchen. "A crash follows this like thunder follows lightning," Dad says back. "I give it a day, maybe less. Hey, you guys looked real good out there today. Ben, that was a very nice catch."

I say thanks, but keep my eye toward the kitchen on

Mom, who's turned it up a notch to Southern Cal or Michigan.

"Don't worry about her," Dad says. "You guys get ready for the dance. I'll take care of this."

Sometimes I don't know whether I want to have my dad canonized or kill him. He weathers these storms like Anderson Cooper on CNN. Just tethers himself to the chair and lets the wind blow. It's like he doesn't care about her, or like he cares too much. You want him to join in or leave. He used to call the doctor at about this point, but Doc would only urge her to take her meds, at which time she would chastise him like a redheaded stepchild. Nothing to do but wait. I'm the only one who still tries to step in, and I only do it when no one else is around.

Cody sees me looking and puts his hand in the middle of my back. "Go get tuxed out," he says. "The fair Miss Suzuki awaits."

He's right. This is not the night to try to repair my mother.

Nine

Here's a good reason for parents and teachers and other concerned adults to encourage teenagers to read: to get the musings of wise dead guys like, say, the poet Robert Burns, who tells us "The best-laid schemes o' mice an' men gang aft agley," which we usually translate into "The best-laid plans of mice and men oft go awry," which I translate into, "The best laid schemes of horny dying short guys oft land in the shitter." The thing I love/hate about life is how an event so sweet it sets a new standard for a good day or even a week can be stuck on the back burner so fast you almost forget it happened.

I pick up Dallas in my newly scrubbed 1941 Chevy pickup, swearing silently to make Coach proud. There is the hope of something soft and warm and torrid as I approach the house. No car is parked outside, and Dallas closes the door too quickly behind her for me to see if her mother and brother are there to spoil any late-night shenanigans.

And she looks *good* in a deep scarlet dress held up by, and only by, two of the three targets of my fantasies since that glorious night in her room, which we haven't talked about since. I am breathless. I've said before she's not beautiful in any classical way, but the entire work of art is, what can I say, a work of art.

We enter the gym to spontaneous applause. It isn't easy to get a good dance crowd in a school of fewer than a hundred kids, so our special dances are open to the entire town; plus, this is homecoming, so there are studs and semistuds from years past and in a couple of instances, decades past. In no one's memory had a homecoming game ever ended the way this one did.

If I could make this night last forever, or at least until I'm outta here, I'd do it, though by cultural homecoming standards it has to appear a little bizarre. The band, if you can call it that, was selected by the juniors, who sponsor the dance to make money for their senior trip next year. To entice the townsfolk they've gone retro, and it's pretty clear their time machine jammed in reverse. The band calls itself "Purple Floyd" and goes back even farther than its pink brother. These guys know Beach Boys songs. And when they break into something faster than "Moonlight Sonata" (only joking; they don't play "Moonlight Sonata"), you look onto the floor and see the entire history of white people dancing (beneath twisted purple and gold crepe paper streamers and tinfoil stars), which in my view is not the part of our history most of us point to with pride.

But if you don't pay attention to all that, if you just enjoy the moment, well, there's a lot to recommend it. Dallas's smooth muscle beneath skin so soft space aliens would kill her for her hide highlights the true meaning of perspective and relativity because, from my point of view, there is simply nothing like her. I know other kids feel the same about people they're with, which is what makes life on earth interesting. I want to be here longer. I am aware that this might very well be the crowning glory of my *life,* as I am aware that I am very old if you count back from my end, rather than up from my birth. I think I am in love, and the idea of losing that love fills me with such deep longing I think I might disappear through the gym floor. Dallas feels none of it, I'm sure.

She's talking to her friends, showing me off, teasing, and I'm smiling and teasing back as if I'm two entities, a young high school kid with his whole life in front of him and an old, old man, staring into the eye of the universe to see who blinks. I feel immortal—that catch today was undoable—and I feel *so* mortal because there will most certainly be nothing else like it. Dancing the slow ones, my head resting lightly against Dallas's breasts, brings thoughts of the feel of that catch on my fingertips. Moments of perfection feel the same no matter the venue.

Paradox runs rampant. I am attached to Dallas as if a chord runs directly through our hearts and I am completely unattached, floating alone through the night, ghostly already. I do not understand because in my mind it is so incongruous, and in my heart completely so. And we have spoken no intimate words.

My brother walks through the door, alone, and the gym explodes into a standing, cheering, *thunderous* ovation. The band stops, then cranks up a rock-and-roll version of our fight song. Guys shake his hand and pound his back. I take Dallas's hand and walk toward him as the crowd parts like the Red Sea. As we walk down the bare seabed my brother opens his arms.

Dallas gently drops my hand and I walk into Cody's embrace. He whispers into my ear, "Don't let 'em shit you, little bro; this one belongs to you. Wherever I go, you go with."

Suddenly I feel Coach behind us, and we've got a little group-hug thing going that we might eat a lot of shit for on Monday but that feels just right in this moment. "You guys enjoy this. It was special out there today. People live their whole lives without feeling this." He's quiet a second, then, "Thanks."

In the parking lot, Dallas sits in the pickup and I'm about to get in the driver's side. Something bigger than a football game has taken over; something even bigger than my desire to get naked and sweaty with a girl who, just this moment, owns me. I'm afraid to get into the pickup and drive away, like I'll break something. Cody slaps my shoulder as he passes toward Dad's car, and as my hand grips the door handle, Coach hollers my name from his car across the lot. I walk toward him and we meet halfway. "I can't keep you out as a starter anymore, Ben. You've put four years into this one. You've earned it. This is a game where, when the stars line up, focus and intention elevate even the most mediocre talent, and somehow you lined yours up and kept them there all year. I'm late getting to this, but it has to happen."

"Naw, Coach," I say. "I—"

"It isn't up to you, Ben. It's done. Everyone thinks that pass today was your brother's doing, and I have no problem giving him his due; Peyton Manning couldn't have laid it in there better. But I don't know two guys in my history as a player or a coach who could have brought that baby home. I know you like to push your brother in front of you, but he doesn't need that. He stands on his own. Today was your day."

Though his voice never breaks, a tear trickles down the inside of Coach's nose. I reach to shake his hand but he disappears into the dark of the parking lot.

On the way back to the pickup I see my brother standing next to Dad's car talking with Sooner. I walk over to say hey, but when Sooner sees me coming he takes off.

My brother shakes his head. I say, "What's up?"

"Fuck," he says. "Sooner came up but he never went inside. He sat out here in his car."

"What?"

"He had a date with a girl from Council, but she stood him up at the last minute. He got here and couldn't make himself go in. Said he didn't deserve it because he wasn't part of the game."

I watch Sooner's taillights as he leaves the lot. "Jeez. Stuff like that happens, makes it hard to hate him."

Cody shakes his head. "The guy's got nothin' but football and his old man steals that from him." He shakes his head again and gets in the car. "Be a good boy," he says, and starts the engine.

I pull the pickup in front of Dallas's house and kill the lights. Her mother's car is nowhere to be seen and the house is dark, save for the single bulb burning on the ceiling of the covered porch. The dim light from the dash casts Dallas in an almost ethereal glow. She turns in the seat and runs her finger the length of my cheek. "Some day, huh, Little Wolf?"

"Some day."

"Wanna come in?"

"I can't tell you."

"Mom and the future Unabomber are at my aunt's; and there's good news and bad news," she says. A slight smile crosses her lips.

"There's *more* good news? Give it to me."

"I want you to stay with me tonight," she says.

What news could be bad in the face of that? I wait.

"We're not having sex."

Oh. Girl knows how to evaluate the news.

There are times when what is, is, whether it seems like it should be or not. One look at Dallas tells me there is no arguing this. And there is no going home. I will stay, and we won't have sex.

And that's not so bad at first. . . .

"Have you thought about the future much?" Dallas says. She's lying beside me in her way-too-big bed in a long T-shirt that isn't supposed to be sexy, but it has her in it. The small night-light by the door casts the room in soft blue, and even her posters of Mia Hamm and Karch Kiraly look sexy. When I dressed tonight I thought I'd be clever, wearing my Captain Underpants under pants beneath my fine-looking burgundy tux. I'm regretting that now, because they are no longer under my burgundy tux and it's possible they make me seem less virile. Truth be told I was hoping by now I wouldn't be wearing them.

"I think about it all the time," I say. "Why?"

"Do you think about me in it?"

I need to be careful here. I like Dallas a lot. A *lot*. But her future and my future are of two different lengths.

"I'm kind of afraid to," I say.

"Really?"

"Yeah, it's complicated, and you're not exactly easy to read. Do you think about me in the future?"

"I wonder about you," she says.

For the first time it occurs to me that one reason I've been so excited about Dallas, besides the obvious one so apparent under that T-shirt, is that in my heart of hearts I thought there was no way she could want anything long-term with me. She's smart and a good enough volleyball player to play at the next level, so her choice of schools will be dictated by recruitment offers. Since I got the Bad News and then the good news from her in the form of an invite to homecoming, I thought she was safe, as in couldn't be hurt. Especially after we slept together and she turned me out into the cold. I already eat shit every day thinking about my brother and my parents. There's nothing I can do about them, though. The universal lottery stuck me with them and vice versa, but time with Dallas is a choice.

"I wonder about you, too," I tell her.

She's quiet a moment, then, "Did you wonder why I slept with you the other night and then turned you out like a stray cat?"

"I was just thinking about that." My head is on her stomach and she's running her fingernails through my hair. "I didn't exactly feel like a stray cat, but yeah, it's usually the guy. . . . Yeah, I wondered."

"Want to know?"

"Um-hmm." Goose bumps pop up on my back like measles as the points of her fingernails glide lightly over my scalp.

She's quiet again. It's a good thing I'm here for the night. This isn't exactly a rapid-fire conversation.

"I was testing."

"Me?"

"Me."

"I don't get it."

Dallas takes a long breath. "I wanted to know if I'd been ruined."

"Ruined?"

She's quiet again, and I'm thinking, I may not have time for this relationship. Literally.

"My uncle . . . I'm not who I appear to be."

I get goose bumps on top of my goose bumps. I watch enough CNN to know what uncles do. "What about him?"

"He . . . he got to me."

"You mean . . . "

She puts a finger to my lips, and whispers, "Yes."

"So you were testing to see . . . "

"If I could still . . . you know."

"Could you?"

"Couldn't you tell?"

"I've heard girls fake it sometimes. You know, to make us feel all manly and shit."

"I like you, Ben. I know about living in secrecy. Secrecy's okay with the general public, but you'd better not be doing it with people you care about. It ruins everything."

Without asking, I assume she's speaking from experience. I said before I'm the go-to guy in a crisis. My panic button and my rage have a delayed reaction. "You want to talk about it?"

"I thought I was talking about it. You mean in detail? No, I do not want to talk about it."

Actually I'm glad, because I don't want to hear it. This will come rushing back over me in the next weeks in that awful wave that comes with the unthinkable. It's threatening right now. I say, "You're safe now, though, right?"

A short laugh. "Yeah, I'm safe now. At least from my uncle."

We lie a long time, quiet. Dallas's fingernails are still absently tracing my scalp and I'm listening to her breathe. Man, those fingers are driving me crazy, but even Sooner would know this is not the time for *any* kind of move.

It's like she's reading my mind. "Don't worry, little man, we'll have more chances."

"What are you doing here?"

"Did you think I lived at your house?" Hey-Soos says.

"I guess I did."

He reaches over and pats my chest. "I live here," he says. I can almost feel his touch physically.

"So," he says, "you rang?"

"Did I?"

"You meant to."

"You mean because of what Dallas said?"

"Duh."

"'Duh?' That's not exactly otherworldly."

"'Duh' is universal. Do you know how many people she's told?"

I say I don't.

"Well," he says, "as she might put it, if she tells one more that will be two."

"No shit?"

"Are you sure that's the way you want to talk to the likes of me?"

"No kidding?"

"No shit," Hey-Soos says. "That's a big truth she told you. You could have jumped up and run. A lot of guys would, or at least slid out the side."

It hadn't even occurred to me. "Really?"

"Look around the locker room sometime."

"So what does it mean?"

"She told you the truth."

"You said that." Hey-Soos looks at me in that way that gives meaning to what they say about the eyes being windows to the soul. I almost can't return his look when he does that, and I get it.

"Oh. The truth. You mean, I should—"

I pop awake. Dallas's head is tucked in the crook of my elbow, her chin resting on my chest. I feel her breath, quiet and even. She is so . . . so beautiful, so inviting. Though I don't even know what he looks like, I can't help picturing her uncle, and my stomach churns. I hear her word: *ruined.* What if she really thinks that?

I said before, I feel like I love her. I don't know what

that means for sure, but it *feels* that way. Not sexual—well, sexual, too—but that's not where the feeling comes from. Hey-Soos is right. I don't know if he's—I'm—right about her not telling anyone else, but most of what he says turns out to be true. If it's right that I'm the only person she's told, that's a lot of trust. I wonder how she knew I wouldn't freak out. Now I have to decide whether or not to tell her the truth about me. I watch her chest rise and fall to her breathing, and almost choke, thinking about it. It would bring great relief to talk to someone in the real world, but I do *not* want people treating me like I'm dying. Nobody. I want to make this year my life: a regular life where people treat you regular. It seems like I have a right to ask for that. I drift again.

"Twice in one night?"

"Slow week. You think you love her."

"Yeah," I say. *"I'm too young to know what love really is."*

"Really?"

"That's, you know, what people say."

"And people *really know what they're talking about, right?"*

"Well, whoever they are, they have a point. I mean, what does somebody like me know about love?"

"There isn't an entity in the universe that does not know about love," Hey-Soos says. "You may be mixing it up with sexual desire, or with some need to make love exclusive of all other people."

"Man, you're working me too hard."

"I'm going to give you one free," he says. "Love, in the universal sense, is unconditional acceptance. In the individual sense, the one-on-one sense, try this: we can say we love each other if my life is better because you're in it and your life is better because I'm in it. The intensity of the love is weighed by how much *better*."

"But what about when you think, you know, you love someone but you have, like, really intense sexual feelings about someone else."

"Don't change the subject. We're talking about love."

I start to ask what's the difference but Hey-Soos raises his hands and shoves her in reverse and—

I am lying in Dallas Suzuki's bed in the early-morning darkness, listening to her easy breathing, knowing full well my life is better because she's in it and wondering if the same will be true if I figure out how in hell I'm going to tell her the truth about myself.

Ten

"You wear that to bed?" Dad asks, nodding at my burgundy tux. It's late Sunday morning and we're at the breakfast table. Cody is still in bed and Mom is crashed in the bedroom.

I smile. The tux is still perfectly pressed; clearly I did not wear it to bed. Dad is practicing facetiousness. Actually he's not practicing; he's been good at it for quite a while. He takes my plate to the stove and piles on scrambled eggs and bacon.

"I paid a lot of money to rent this," I say. "Wanted my money's worth."

"It seems you didn't come home last night."

I look down at the tux. "It does seem like that."

"Your mother was going to stay up and have a talk with you."

I cringe at the thought. *That* would have been a long talk.

"The last thing she said before she cashed it in was that I should have it with you."

"The talk? Is it the one she wanted you to have with Cody when he was fourteen?"

He scratches his chin and smiles. "That's the one."

I laugh. "You're in the clear. I had it with Cody."

"She's worried . . . "

"That I'm going to get a girl pregnant and throw away my chances for a long, lustrous career as a jockey?"

I pick at my food. Eggs and bacon are not part of my preferred diet, but I don't necessarily want Dad to know that. I'll make myself some oatmeal later. I pretend to eat as I lay out the stats from the Planned Parenthood website. Rote. I can't bring any surprises into my own life that will have lasting effect, 'cause I won't be lasting, but I'm not about to complicate Dallas's life, either. "I'll spare you the gory details, Dad, but anybody who doesn't use protection is an unconscious dick. And if it helps, the protection I used last night was abstinence."

"'Nuff said," he says, looking relieved. My dad does a pretty good job with Cody and me when it comes to problem solving, but he does *not* address the sexual or the emotional with great confidence.

And like I said, I didn't do anything last night with Dallas that could relegate us to a single-wide trailer for the next thirty years. But I don't care. I'm hooked and wherever it goes I'm going with it. I can close my eyes in the privacy of my room and go back to that first night with her any time I get a hankerin'. I look at Mom's closed bedroom door. "Are you leaving next year after we're gone?"

Dad looks at me like I'm speaking Russian.

"You know, when we're off to college."

"Yeah, I know when you're off to college. Listen Ben, it may not look like your mother and I have much together, and compared to some folks we probably don't. But there was a time, and twenty years ago I made a deal. I'll admit it would have been hard to wrap my imagination around the *worse* in *for better or worse*, but I made a deal. I don't shoot a horse with a broken leg and I don't turn my back when someone I care about gets sick. Your mother's sick."

"I just meant I wouldn't blame you. I mean,

sometimes I remember a whole different person when we were little. You could talk to her. She had fun. It's like you can't connect with her anymore. If somebody asked me what my mother's like, I wouldn't know what to say, other than she's going a hundred or she's parked."

"Son, do you know what it must feel like to live inside her body? Inside her head?" He shakes his head. "No, I made a deal, Ben." And the conversation is closed.

That's one reason I don't tell him. He made a deal about me, too.

Early October

I'm feeling more and more like I need to hold Lambeer's feet to the fire. I've figured out that if you're a teacher you can say anything about any damn thing you want, and if no one challenges you, it becomes fact. Now this puts me behind the curve a ways, but the more I put Malcolm X's perspectives alongside the information in *Lies My Teacher Told Me*, the brasher a student I become. Like I said earlier, according to Loewen, what you read in any American history textbook is pretty much 130 to 150 percent bullshit. They get the names right and they know the War of 1812 started in 1812, but the stuff they leave out turns almost any high school history book into an eight-hundred-page infomercial for the good ol' U. S. of A. As was said about Andrew Jackson's policies, "To the victor belong the spoils," which among other things means those in power get to write history. It isn't much of a jump to believe that spills over into our U.S. government textbooks.

So I figure I owe it to myself and to my classmates, who have never failed to join me in my relentless quest to keep Lambeer off-topic, to bring my newfound knowledge into the learning factory.

"Mr. Wolf the Lesser," Lambeer says at the opening bell, "you said you would choose your term project by today. Are you ready?"

"Yes, Your Honor, I am," I say back.

"And your project will be . . . "

"To follow the prescribed local political process and get the city council to name a street after Malcolm X."

"What?"

"To follow the prescribed–"

"I heard you, Mr. Wolf. I'm afraid that won't do. At the very least Malcolm X belongs in a history class, and I'm hard pressed to say he belongs there."

"Au contraire," I say. "It will have to do. I've already

started the wheels rolling. I can't stop them. It's bigger than both of us, sir."

That gets a few laughs. Sooner says, "Jesus, Wolf. You see any black dudes in this school?"

For maybe the first or second time in his life, Sooner Cowans has a point. But so do I. "Nope, I do not see any black dudes or dudettes. But there are streets in every town in this country named after white heroes that have nothing but black or Latino or Asian folks on them, and we don't think a thing about that. I'm simply making a modest push for equality, which my textbook tells me is also the goal of our government. That makes it current and definitely about government and therefore appropriate for this class."

Dallas says, "Right on, Little Wolf."

Cody lightly bangs his forehead on his desktop.

Lambeer says, "Mr. Wolf, are you doing this to get attention?"

"The only way I'll get attention is if you don't let me do it," I say back. "Except for the people who are working together, I'll bet there aren't three kids in here who could tell you what any other kid's project is. Shoot, I don't even know what Cody's doing."

That gives Lambeer pause. He may be the Bill

O'Reilly of social studies teachers, but, unlike with O'Reilly, if you make sense you can usually get a break. "It sounds pretty frivolous," he says, "but I'll give it some consideration."

"So how come we didn't study Malcolm X in history?" It's two days later and I've had time to read a little more of Loewen's book and a little more *Malcolm X* and become even more indignant about my education.

"I'd like to discuss this with you, Mr. Wolf," Lambeer says, "but as I said, this is current events and Malcolm X has been dead around forty years."

Sooner says, "Jesus, Wolf, give it a rest. Go see the movie."

"Matter of fact, I did see the movie. Denzel Washington *was* Malcolm. Wonder why he didn't win the Oscar for it."

Lambeer says, "Are you saying it was because he was black?"

"Geez," I say, "I never thought of *that.*"

"I'm going to put this to sleep, Mr. Wolf. I went back through my last year's U.S. history notes and as a matter of fact I did mention Mr. X in two lectures. There are limits to what you can cover in the short period of two semesters. Now if that didn't meet your standards, I'm sorry, but we must move on. And I have to tell you, I've decided to put your Malcolm X street-naming project out of range. The truth is, the school has a levy to pass this year and if you're canvassing for something that frivolous, we could lose that levy. So select another project."

"You're going to sabotage my education for a few bucks?" I say with exaggerated disbelief. "Does Idaho have an ACLU?"

"ACLU is in California, you dip-shit," Sooner says.

Dallas says, "That's UCLA, Sooner. Every state has an ACLU."

"Well, pardon *me*," Sooner says back. I am single-handedly driving this class out of control.

Lambeer raises his hand high, supposedly a signal for all to fall silent. "That's enough! Now let's get this class back on track."

But I have been armed by James Loewen. "Did you know that when it came to the indigenous populations of the West Indies and Haiti, Christopher Columbus had about the same sensibilities as Adolf Hitler? How come you didn't teach us that in U.S. history?"

"Mr. Wolf, I'll say it one more time. This class is about United States government and current events. If you took issue with my history curriculum you should have said it back then."

I'm on a roll. "Okay, then how come you haven't told us about the Native American influence on the ideas put forth in the Constitution, and particularly on the Bill of Rights?"

Dolven says, "Jesus, Wolf, did you whack your head against the goalposts when you dove for that catch?"

I spend the last half hour of class in enforced silence.

"Which of our quiet tree-lined streets did you have pegged for Malcolm X Avenue, little big bro," Cody says in the lunchroom, "before your noble project was quashed?"

My brother mocks me. The only paved street in Trout is Main Street and it's only paved because it's the single state highway connecting north and south Idaho. The temperatures in this place get so cold then warm up so quickly that we get serious *frost heaves*, where the moisture beneath the road freezes, then turns to oozing mud pushing up through in the springtime. We call the big ones *jelly rolls*, and when they start to show in the spring, little kids go out and bounce on them to soften them up even more. There are urban myths—or maybe rural myths—of kids getting sucked into the mud and going down like a bad guy in the quicksand of an old Tarzan movie. At any rate, if you were to pave those streets, the frost heaves would only buckle the pavement and cost the taxpayers more money than a school levy. My Malcolm X Avenue would not exactly be a quiet suburban tree-lined street.

"I was just making a point," I tell my brother now. "We live in a country where racism and divisiveness and ignorance and fear rule the day. It's so bad, there are things that happened four hundred years ago they're afraid to tell us about today. Just because we live in Podunk, Idaho, where it's easy not to pay any attention to all that, doesn't mean we're not going to get confronted with it when we get out in the world."

"Man, who have you been talking to? What you need to pay attention to is getting behind the quarterback who's taking us to State. Wipe your mind clear of your lofty thoughts, my older, smaller, cerebral sib, and pay attention to what matters. You'll have plenty of time for social work when the season's over."

"You're right," I say, but I'm thinking I don't have plenty of time for anything.

● ● ●

There's an envelope with my name on it taped to Marla's door when I arrive after practice for my appointment, next to a typed notice declaring all appointments canceled for the week. Someone will be in touch by phone or e-mail. I open the note.

Ben,

I'm sorry, I can't do this. I thought I could but I can't. My favorite professor at the university said he gets his best piece of therapeutic information every time he boards an airplane. The flight attendant says if the oxygen mask drops down, be sure to put on your own before helping anyone with theirs. I'm afraid I haven't put mine on. It hurts too much to talk to you. It's not your fault.

Marla

That's a different way of looking at the oxygen mask dropping. Dang! Too many issues for a *therapist*! That should come with an award. It also sucks. I'm assuming the someone who will be in touch will be a new therapist, which I don't like much. I was just breaking Marla in, and she wasn't scary to talk to. It was nice having someone besides Hey-Soos, who I still suspicion is Ben Wolf in a bathrobe, to talk with. I shouldn't have teased her so much. I feel sorry, I feel bad, and just a little pissed. I thought if you graduated from therapy school, you had that shit down.

What the hell, maybe I don't need therapy. I mean, who knows more about me than me? Hey-Soos, maybe, but who *real*? What I need is to get on with things. I need to rattle some cages. That's why football feels so good, I think. I can make people listen. I don't try to make somebody walk away *hurt* from a hit by me. I just want them to know I need to be dealt with.

"Tell me all you know about Malcolm X."

"I'm depending on my memory," Rudy says. "Not good."

"He made the pilgrimage to Mecca, right? Is that, like, the same Islam we're dealing with today? Guys beheading people and shit?"

"You can't judge Islam by those people any more than you can judge Christians by abortion clinic bombers or white separatists. Love turns to hate at the fringes of any belief system." Rudy sounds like a college prof. I don't see the half-empty bottle inside a paper sack on the tool bench these days. He's almost cleaned up, there's a whiff of Old Spice, and I've noticed the supplements dwindling. He's like a whole new resource in my war for an education, plus he was a *priest*. What more could you ask for when you're on your way out? I mean, Catholic priests are supposed to have a line to the Big Guy, straight through the Pope. That doesn't jibe with Hey-Soos's grasp of things, but nothing wrong with getting divergent views.

"So what *about* guys who bomb abortion clinics?" I ask him. "Catholics are big-time against abortion."

"Guys who bomb abortion clinics are murderers," he says, "and I'm not a priest anymore, or even a Catholic. Even when I was, I thought guys who bomb abortion clinics are murderers."

"How come you left the church?" I've asked it before.

He shakes his head. "Don't go there. I've told you before—"

I raise my hands in surrender. "I got it," I say. "I just get interested in stuff. So were you thinking of following Malcolm X?"

"No, I wasn't thinking of following Malcolm X, and he certainly wouldn't have invited me to. I just got interested in his perspectives when I read Haley's book. I was questioning, and I liked the way he questioned."

That's what I'm into. Questioning. It's how you learn. Even when you don't get the answers, you get the heat to find them. Right now my heat is turned on high.

"Like I said before," Rudy says, "it's all about differences. Something about humans really doesn't like them, when they are the very thing we should embrace. If someone's different from you and it scares you or makes you mad, that's God telling you to take a closer look. If you're scared or mad, that's about you, not about the person who scares or angers you." He looks at his watch. "Don't you have a curfew?"

"Yeah."

"What time?"

"Ten."

"You're past it. Get out of here."

"Coach doesn't really enforce it."

"Get out of here anyway. I'm tired. And you ask too many questions."

Rudy doesn't want to get out of practice being the town drunk, even when he isn't drinking. He is one interesting guy.

Eleven

"How come you haven't pushed me to get treatment?"

"Not my job," Hey-Soos says.

"Some guardian angel or whatever you are. You don't care if I live or die."

"That's because I know nothing dies," he says. "Things change. You're choosing change."

"Another thing I'm way not smart enough to say! Or even think. Where is this craziness coming from?"

"Just listen to yourself."

"I'm scared."

"I know. You can still choose treatment."

"I'd just get bald and sick and die anyway."

"I have nothing against going with instinct."

"So how did I know?"

"I don't know for sure that you did, but sometimes we're privy to information that comes through senses other than our brains."

In that space in my brain or my heart or maybe the landscape exactly between, Hey-Soos and I just look at each other. Finally I say, "You willing to tell me some stuff?"

"You mean, like secrets of the universe?"

"Yeah, like that."

"Try me," he says.

"Why am I here? I mean, what's the purpose if I'm gonna be gone so quick? It's not like anybody's going to listen to me; I'm just going to be this small guy who had a good year on the football field. The good citizens of Trout aren't really going to name a street after Malcolm X. My mother won't get healed knowing me. My brother won't all of a sudden learn to decipher defenses. And Dallas . . . God, Dallas."

"You're asking the purpose of life."

"I'm asking the purpose of my life."

"I'll tell you all you need to know. Look, I'm a scientist. Everything out here in the universe came from a single thing, something scientists call the big bang. That means you have within you everything the universe has within it. When you know something without learning it, it's because some part of you connects up with something out there and it is familiar.

You know it without learning it. That's just a side effect. The point is that everything that exists inside you also exists outside you. The world is practice for the inner you.

"Think of life on earth as a video game. A serious one, one you are totally drawn to. While you're playing that game you don't pay attention to anyone or anything else. You're sucked in. You learn the rules and follow them to a tee because you know if you don't, you're out of the game. You get excited. You get disappointed; you get pissed. Everything is focused on continued play. Play the game once and you might last a long time, but play it again and you might get taken out early because something in the game jumped up and bit you in the ass."

"Like disease?"

"Like disease. But even when you see it jump up and bite you and you know you're going down, you stay with it and get as many points as you can; that is, if you have proper reverence for the game."

"That's what I'm doing now?"

"And if you're playing it with someone else, they get better because you do your best and they try to stay with you. You get more and more focused and you discover things you didn't know about the game before because it allows you to get more points, to go as far as you can."

"I think I get it."

"I think you do, too," Hey-Soos says. "So don't worry about your brother and his college football career, or Dallas, or whether you can make your mother okay. If you play the game the best you can, you have the best chance of others seeing a piece of what you see."

That seems like what should be the end of a Conversation with Hey-Soos, but he doesn't back up and I don't wake up.

I say, "What about Rudy?

"Case in point. Not exactly what you expected, is he?"

"That's an understatement."

"Maybe he needs something from you, too. And if you want a little piece of information that will let you cut to the chase quicker, just remember, no one is."

"No one is what?"

"What you expect. I mean, what do you imagine people think when they first see you coming at them on an open football field?"

"Yeah, I'm—"

"Not what they expect."

Early November

Football gets a little tougher as the season wears on. Earlier on, in late summer and early fall days, we practice in seventy, sometimes eighty degrees, nearly always under deep blue mountain skies. I forget sometimes what a stunning part of the country I live in. But the only thing shorter than Indian summer around here is me, and by this time of year we're Googling our laptops for imminent snow, or worse, miserable cold rain. We got through Halloween with none of the white stuff and I'm hoping Thanksgiving, which means through the football season, but it doesn't look good. I've run a few cross-country meets in whiteouts but no one was trying to knock me down.

And we have turned it up a notch when I didn't think there were more notches. We haven't had a tough game since Horseshoe Bend. Win one more, we go to Regionals; one more after that, we go to State. Coach is playing it cool but you can tell he wants it like nothing else because with every mental error we run wind sprints like someone just screamed, "Tsunami."

"If you're overmatched physically, blame God," Coach hollers over and over, "but mental alertness belongs to *you*!" We're gonna be sharp and we're gonna be in killer shape. Should we live.

After Monday's practice, Coach calls me into his room off the lockers. "Hey, little big man, you caught a couple of sweet ones out there today."

"My brother was putting them where I couldn't miss."

"Is he doing okay? Anything going on I should know?"

"Not that I know of. Why?"

"Just keeping my fingers in all the pies," he says. "He looks great to me, but you'd be the first person to see any cracks. A lot rides on these next games."

"No kidding," I say. "Lose one and you're a spectator."

"I mean for your brother. Scouts at every game. He should come out of this with a full ride. Your brother can be a hell of a college quarterback and he can get a good education in the bargain. I know your parents are going to be strapped sending the two of you off next year. Cody shows his best stuff these last games and that covers books and tuition for one."

Coach is telling *me* this because he doesn't want to pressure Cody.

"My brother's set, Coach. I mean he's still dyslexic reading defenses, but that's business as usual."

Coach smiles. "Swear to God, half that scholarship should be yours, buddy. You may be smaller, but that's just physical size."

"Cody'll be okay."

"And how about you?"

"What do you mean?"

"Been hearing rumors about you in Lambeer's class."

"Aw, I'm just keeping Mr. Lambeer honest. He acts like he *wrote* history, or at least the Constitution."

"Well, don't mess with him too much. He's been known to use grades as a weapon, and I'll deny I said that."

"All I need is a D minus."

Coach laughs. "Okay, let me know when I need to prepare to bail you out."

If you're playing high school football at any level, and you're a couple of games away from winning the state championship, your head and heart are full. I have a feeling it's that way when you get toward the top of anything. You're part of something and if you do everything you can with whatever talent you have, it's almost spiritual. Football in this country gets a bad rap sometimes, I think, because of its press: big, tough, seriously uncerebral. That might be because the first guys who got hold of the game didn't know what they had, or how to treat it. You can make the standard case against it, that your body wasn't meant to be treated that way, that if you do it long and hard enough you'll wind up with bad knees and/or bad ankles and/or a loose brain. All that's correct, but once you make the contract to play, then it's all about you and your teammates.

Doesn't matter if they're your friends or not; if you want the unit to work, the "thing" that is all of you, then you play in concert with one another. I mean, I don't care how smart I am about angles and seeing ahead and surprising guys by concentrating all my energy on one point when I hit them; if my guys don't knock a whole bunch of people down before I get there, I don't get there. Many things happened between the moment the ball was hiked and the moment that sweet pigskin settled onto my fingertips in the Horseshoe Bend game. Cecil Cross is probably the least talented starter on the team. I'll bet I haven't even mentioned him. He works his ass off every practice, runs sprints till he pukes, and works on his moves like a ballerina, but the only thing he lacks more than coordination is strength. He starts at offensive guard, and when you watch the tapes of that last touchdown, he's so overmatched, he might as well be Richard Simmons in the ring with Muhammad Ali. He's taking forearms to the helmet and getting shoved back and to the side by a guy with twice his skills, but ol' Cecil stays between his assailant and Cody long enough for Cody to get the ball off. If Cecil blows it, Cody is on his back. But Cecil *doesn't* blow it and the ball settles into my outstretched hands. Nobody cheered and stomped when Cecil Cross walked into the dance that night, but we're a team and Cecil did his job and every guy knows it.

My point is there are a lot of rewards for doing it right and the big one could be a state championship. But it's part of a bigger thing for me. When that ball floated into my hands it felt like the *truth*. I would be there, Cody would put it there, and all I had to do was hold on. It almost made me understand why some guys point to the sky when they make a good play, like God wanted them to catch it or something, which by the way, really pisses me off when I see it. I like Hey-Soos's take on things. I'd be real worried about a big bang God who gave a shit about a football game. But when you do everything right, and it works, it feels somehow *elevated*. Given my condition, I work for that feeling every play of every practice. I want one more catch like the Horseshoe Bend catch.

I've been going over to Dallas's place almost every night after practice, hanging out with her and her little brother. Mrs. Suzuki seems to like me well enough, but disappears into the kitchen or the bedroom shortly after I arrive. She's hard to read; I can't tell if she's "giving us space" or if she's just uncomfortable. She and Dallas don't look at all alike, partially because she supplies the Caucasian half of Dallas's DNA and partially because she's at least five inches shorter. But like I said, she's nice to me and she feeds me, so I'm happy.

Dallas wrapped up her volleyball season a week ago when they got knocked out of the district tournament the first day. (Don't think she wasn't a little hard to communicate with after that happened.) She gets a couple of weeks before basketball and her after-school time is focused on Joe Henry, who is one of the most compelling little dudes you would care to meet. He's four plus with shoulder-length shiny black hair and horn-rimmed specs that make him look like a thirty-year-old little person. Today I knock and look through the window. Dallas is sitting on the floor cross-legged with Joe Henry perched on her knees. Dallas waves me in without turning around. She and Joe Henry are staring into each other's eyes, laughing, paying me no attention. I smell roast beef cooking.

"You can lead a horse to water . . . " Dallas says.

"But you don't can make him do push-ups," Joe Henry finishes, then laughs like a maniac.

"A bird in the hand . . . "

"Gets squoze." More laughter.

"Hickory dickory dock . . . " Dallas says.

"Two mouses ran up the clock."

"Mice."

"Right," Joe Henry says. "Mice."

"The clock struck one . . . " Dallas says.

"And the other one escraped with minor injuries."

"Escaped, not 'escraped.'"

"Yeah, that. Do another one."

"Little Miss Muffet, sat on a tuffet . . . "

"I like this one," Joe Henry says. "Eating her curds away. . . "

"It's curds and whey. Two words. Say it. Curds and whey."

"Curds and whey. Go!"

"Along came a spider," Dallas says, "and sat down beside her and said . . . "

"Is this seat taken?" Joe Henry goes into convulsions.

I step inside the screen door and let it close loudly. "You guys taking that act on the road?"

"Soon as Joe Henry gets his part down," Dallas says. Without putting her hands on the floor, she stands from the cross-legged position, walks over, and kisses me lightly on the mouth, then on the cheek.

"Your mom around?" I ask, hoping the opposite, though it doesn't matter because of Joe Henry.

Dallas nods toward the kitchen. "Smell that dinner cooking? You think *I'm* cooking that?"

"Ask me what's inside my sleeping bag," Joe Henry says to me.

"What?"

He frowns at Dallas. She says, "Ask him what's inside his sleeping bag."

I squat to his eye level, which isn't far for me. "What's inside your sleeping bag, Joe Henry?"

"Duck down!" he screams and ducks down, then falls to the floor, rolling over and over.

Jeez. "If my eyes rolled back any farther in my head and I started to cry the tears would run down my back," I tell them.

Joe Henry squeals. "Tears down my back," he says.

I go for the kill. "They'd call it back-tear-ia."

Joe Henry stares at me.

"Jesus," Dallas says and wrinkles her nose. "Jesus, Ben. That's bad. You can be arrested for telling a joke like that."

"Bacteria," I say to Joe Henry.

Dallas says, "Jesus, Ben."

Joe Henry says, "Jesus, Ben."

Hey, look what I had to work with.

Before the night's over I've got Joe Henry running

the exact patterns I'll run for the next two weeks, and his Nerf football bounces off every part of his body but his hands. But brings the ball back time after time and I get the sense he could catch his first pass any day now. Dallas watches and smiles.

At the door she kisses me longer; sweet.

"What a great kid," I tell her.

"You like my guy? He has his days." She looks back over her shoulder at Joe Henry who lies on the floor, holding the Nerf football like a pillow, passed out. "From sixty to zero in five seconds," she says. "Get out of here. We have school tomorrow."

"I'm glad football players don't have to turn in homework," I say.

"Football players *do* have to turn in their home-work," she says. "At this school V-ballers rule."

I look at my watch. Man, I don't want to leave. But . . . "If that's the case," I say, "I'd better go do some. It will be the first this week."

She laughs. "You can bring us all up to date on Malcolm X," she says. "Jeez, Ben."

"Hey, I wasn't kidding. Malcolm was a righteous dude."

"Whatever you say."

* * *

A dim light glows through the living room window as I pull up to the house, which means Dad is kicked back in his recliner plowing through *Team of Rivals,* Doris Kearns Goodwin's biography of Lincoln. When my dad's not at work or dozing, he reads. I say hi and cross the room toward the stairs. Dad doesn't like to be jerked away from a good book and he looks comfortable in his recliner that's way too big for our living room.

"Hey, Ben?"

I'm halfway up the stairs. "Yeah?"

"Is there something I should know about?"

My heart jumps. "Like what?"

"I don't know," he says. "You've been . . . different lately."

"Different? How have I been different?"

"Calmer, I guess. More focused. That's relative, of course. Since about the time you turned out for football, if memory serves. Last couple of years, you were the fart on the proverbial skillet. What's going on?"

Dad's not the first person to notice. Cody rides me all the time about going down to see Rudy, especially since Rudy's been almost conscious and interesting and I lose track of time listening to him. And lots of people ride me when I can't keep my mouth shut about Malcolm X in Current Events. But they'll make a lot of guesses before they suspect the Death Train, so I'm safe. "It's child development, Dad. Maturation. It happens to the worst of us."

He places his book in his lap and studies me, so I sit on the step. "I worry sometimes," he says. "With your mom and all. I've not always paid the best attention. I know she focuses on you; that you don't have the good sense to stay away when she's ready to crash."

"Yeah, but you're the one who takes care of her after she does. I'm okay, Dad. I'm learning about that. I'm getting better." He watches me a few more seconds, then picks up his book.

I think Doc Wagner lets me get away with this charade because he knows what knowledge of my impending death would do to my mom. He knows I wouldn't really sue him for breaking confidentiality. The way I figure it, when I die Mom can grieve the incident and survive that one big hit, but if she had to care for me in her roller coaster condition, the guilt might eat her up. I have an idea that's Doc's thinking, too. Either way, it's gonna hit her like a sledgehammer.

Twelve

One class we don't get a break on during football season is Coach's. As intense as he is on the field, that's how intense he is as a teacher. "Football is a game," he says, "but your education is your life." So we're sitting in his Literature That Means Something class. It's an elective and I think he created it partially to offset Current Events. Lambeer is a teacher who cares *what* you think. Coach cares *how* you think. The class focuses on fiction, but if you can make a case for the literary value of any non-fiction book, he'll give you credit. Then you have to make a class presentation sometime during the quarter and the more discussion you generate, the better your grade. He warns you when you sign up that you'd better be serious.

"There are advantages to attending a small school,"

he said a few months ago on the first day of class. "Small classes, lots of individual attention, all that. But subject material is necessarily limited and if you get a bad teacher for, say English, you've got him four years and there's no escape. By the way, if you happen to think *you* got a bad teacher for English, I encourage you to keep it to yourself. The most important commodity you can take on to college with you is the ability to think logically, to organize your ideas and present them orally or on paper. Learn to do that and you'll fool a lot of profs. I'm tempted to say you'll thank me for putting you through what I'm going to put you through in this class, but you are teenagers, subhuman forms that don't thank anyone for anything until it's way too late. Just kidding."

So today I have my hand in the air because I haven't had a lot of luck getting my point of view across in Lambeer's class. "I want to change my book to *The Autobiography of Malcolm X*." There is a collective groan, not for any bias against Malcolm, I think, but for the repetition.

Coach smiles. "Like I told you earlier, I've heard about your obsession with Malcolm."

"What? Where did you hear that? What obsession?

It's not an obsession. Malcolm is my life. I live and breathe Malcolm. But it's not an obsession."

"In the teachers' lounge," he says. "Mr. Lambeer tells me you're trying to hijack the curriculum."

"Well, it ain't working," I say, "so I'll try here."

"There is no curriculum here," Coach says.

"Which makes it all the easier to hijack."

"Might I remind you," he says, "that *The Autobiography of Malcolm X* is close to five hundred pages? We're over halfway through the semester. You're going to have to read like the wind. What were you reading? David Sedaris, right? You sure you want to give that up?"

I don't tell Coach I'm *re*reading *Malcolm X* so it won't take that long. He's right: I was reading Sedaris, because I consider him a true American. First of all he's, like, as funny as they get, and he's a gay guy who just stands up and says he's gay and writes right on past you if you have that bias, and he teaches you that humans are humans and funny is funny, and I picked him because I needed as much laughter as I could get. But I'll read *him* anyway. Rudy is translating *Malcolm* into real time, so I might as well milk it for all its worth.

"I don't think anyone in this school should be allowed to read that book," Sylvia Longley says.

Coach says, "I'll be sure you're not required to read it."

It's hard to take Sylvia seriously. She's pretty smart, but she's waiting patiently for her first original thought, and while she's waiting, she gives her dad's. He's the state senator from our county and to him, intellectual freedom is the freedom to believe what *he* believes. If he didn't already have a job he could be Lambeer's teaching partner. The scariest part about him, according to my dad, is that he gets elected. "You *couldn't* require me to read it," she says. Sylvia has down that nose-turned-up, lips-slightly-parted, tongue-smacking thing like she invented it.

"Nor would I try," Coach says. "And because we live in a democracy, you couldn't require that anyone else *not* read it." That's what I like about Coach as a teacher, and as a coach for that matter: he doesn't feel the need to accommodate a dumb idea on the off chance that not doing so would bruise some kid's psyche.

"Burning books is not such a bad idea," Sylvia says. "I can't believe this country. It's okay to burn an American flag, but it's not okay to burn some book that's full of trash."

I can hear my brother shaking his head from across

the room. "What's trashy about *Malcolm X*?" he says. "Jeez, Sylvia. Tap your helmet."

"Have you seen the language in that book?" she says.

"I sure as shit have," Cody says, and pauses for the laugh.

Coach says, "Careful there, Golden Boy."

Cody raises his hands in surrender.

"He just makes my point," Sylvia says. "You won't let him use that language in class, but you'll allow a book with ten times worse language in it. That's hypocritical."

"Not really," Coach says. "The language in a book represents the time and conditions. It's history. And the only reason I don't let him use it in class is I don't want someone complaining to Mr. Phelps. Personally I don't care about that language one way or the other. Mr. Wolf said that word loud and clear and I don't see one student bleeding. I'm just following the rules so I can keep my job and win football games."

"I'll say it again," Sylvia says. "We can burn the flag; we should be able to burn books."

Coach stands up. "You know what? You're right. Let's do it." He starts for the door.

We sit, watching.

"Come *on*," he says. "Sylvia's right. We can burn the flag; we can burn a book."

My brother says, "Can we burn a witch?"

Sylvia glares at him like a viper.

"If we can find one who doesn't mind," Coach says. "Let's go."

In the library, Coach marches directly to the shelf where *Malcolm* resides, snags a copy, and walks to the desk while our entire class watches from the hall. Suzy March, the student librarian this period, says, "You don't have to check it out, Mr. Banks. I know you'll bring it back."

Coach pulls out his wallet and hands her a ten. "Actually I won't be bringing this one back," he says, and we disappear down the hall while Suzy stares at Alexander Hamilton.

Out on the front lawn Coach breaks a few small dead branches off a tree, makes a tepee with them, gathers us close to block the chilly late-fall wind. When he gets a little fire he adds the first three or four pages of *Malcolm*. *Malcolm* is quite flammable. He rips out some more pages and lays them on one by one. When it's going good, he puts the rest of the book on. *Malcolm* goes up in smoke in no time flat.

"There," Coach says as the flames burn down. "We said what we had to say about *The Autobiography of Malcolm X.* I feel good. How about you guys?"

"Pretty funny," Sylvia says. "A lot of good that did. There are three more copies in the library and you paid for that one. They can just buy another one."

"You want to burn them all?" Coach says in mock surprise. "Oh, that's different. I don't think I can get behind that. I mean, when somebody burns a flag, they just burn one or maybe a couple. They don't try to burn them all."

"You can say what you want, Mr. Banks, but what's in some books is poison. There have to be books that you think are trash, too. I mean you might not say that to us, but you know it's true."

"You're wrong," Coach says. "I would say it to you. There are a lot of books I think are trash. There are a lot of books I wouldn't recommend to anyone. I mean, there's a book in the Old Testament—which if memory serves from the last state senate campaign, is a big book in your house—that says we're supposed to kill active homosexuals. My younger sister is a homosexual. Active, I think." He waves his hand over our little band of book burners. "And if statistics bear out, so are one and a half of you guys. It just doesn't seem right to kill you."

"This is so stupid," Sylvia says, but Coach ignores her.

"But I don't want the Old Testament banned," he says, "for two reasons. I don't want a bunch of parents coming after me in the middle of the night with torches, and more important, I'm pretty sure you can read that book and not go out and kill homosexuals, because you have other information that tells you that's not okay and because you have a brain."

Sylvia is stomping away by this time and Coach just lets her go. He probably feels bad for embarrassing her, but it was a good lesson. "I suppose now one or two of you will want to burn a flag, but I'm going to have to let you do that on your own and I'd appreciate it if you'd do it off school grounds because I'm going to have a hard enough time explaining *this* to Mr. Phelps at the next teachers' meeting."

"Hey-Soos. Good to see you."

"You too, my friend."

"You check out the book burning today?"

"Your coach knows how to make a point."

"Sylvia Longley," I say. "She looks good, but man, she could give you a permanent headache."

"Sylvia's playing the game the best way she knows how," he says.

"Just seems like she'd be smarter."

"She's plenty smart. She's just scared. The boogeyman in her game is loss of control. It's easy to get on her case, but if Sylvia Longley gives up her belief, she risks losing her dad. Most of us would burn a few books to keep that from happening."

"So I should have agreed with her?"

"I didn't say that. What makes this game interesting is that it's interactive. You have to deal with the Sylvia Longleys of the universe and she has to deal with the Ben Wolfs. Everyone gets a set of controls when they walk on."

I change the subject. "I kind of miss Marla."

"She was a nice young woman. What do you miss?"

"You know, someone to talk to; that I could tell everything."

"You have the Great Confessor in your bedroom and you need someone to talk to?"

"I'm talking about someone real."

"If you prick me, do I not bleed?"

"I can't prick you to find out."

He turns his palms toward me. Bright red blood trickles from scars on each palm.

"Jesus, Hey-Soos. Don't do that. It's creepy."

He laughs. "I love that trick."

"It's not a trick when you're in somebody's dream. Anybody can do anything in a dream. And what's with the scars on your palms? Are you trying to tell me you're really—"

"Naw," he says, "I'm just messin' with you. So what would you talk with Marla about that you can't tell me?"

I get that if I say it, I throw us into a paradox. "Nothing that I can't tell you, really. I've been messing with Lambeer about Malcolm X, but I'm really interested."

"Very misunderstood guy in your culture."

"Rudy says the same thing. He's turning into a whole different guy off the sauce, by the way."

"You had a lot to do with that, you know," Hey-Soos says.

"Yeah," I say. "Me and the nutrients."

"You and your company," he says. "When there's no connection, people die. Malcolm X is probably a pretty good meeting point for the two of you."

"Well, as you can probably tell from a universe away, I'm nuts about Dallas. She's . . . it's like I couldn't have imagined her. I couldn't have dreamed her up to want her. She's tough and she's sad . . . and you should see her with her little brother."

He smiles.

"Right. You have."

"I'm worried. I think she might really like me, like want to spend time with me even after graduation. And . . . well, I'm not gonna be around and . . . "

"You're worried about her expectations."

"Yeah."

"Maybe you should tell her," he says.

"I've thought about it. But man, once people know . . . nothing will be the same. What really worries me is that she feels big-time betrayed by her uncle and all the people who were supposed to take care of her. If she finds out I lied now . . . "

"Ben."

"You're right. She finds out at some point anyway. And whether I'm alive or not, she feels betrayed."

"And if you're not alive . . . "

"She never hears why. God, even in my dreams I'm getting dilemmas I can't solve. She's worried she's ruined."

"By her uncle. But we both know that can't happen, right? People don't get ruined like that, awful as that is. The only truly ruined people are those who believe they are."

"That can't be right."

"Ah, but it can."

"I can't believe that." I look at him harshly.

"What if you lived in a culture where every father had

sexual relations with every daughter before the age of ten? What if it was just what was done? What if you were considered a horrible parent if you didn't do that, and would lose your child? What if every girl in the world was chastised if she missed that coming-of-age event?"

My mind spins.

"Or what if it was to be done by the oldest uncle, as it happened to your friend? What if only girls who had not *had that experience were put on the outside?"*

Even in my dream, I am silent.

"Don't get this wrong, Ben; you don't have time. That is a hugely challenging event for Dallas Suzuki. Because it is a secret and it carries seeming *awfulness, it keeps her from telling the truth. People who feel ruined, or scared all the time, simply can't tell the truth. When she can tell it, own it instead of letting it own her, she'll be fine."*

"So I'm supposed to go to Dallas and say, like, 'Let's have sex. There's nothing wrong with you; it's only in your head'?"

Hey-Soos laughs big. "If you want her to hand you yours. You're not supposed to tell her anything. You're supposed to make sure you never treat her as if she's ruined."

And if I don't tell her the truth about myself, I'm treating her as if she's ruined; as if she can't take it.

Hey-Soos says, "So what else?" It's like he's doing this

inventory, reminding me I have limited time.

"Football's going good," I say finally. "Coach keeps telling us our only job is to make sure we leave nothing on the field in these last two games. I've got my brother up to speed on our next opponent, Timberline, who could take us without Sooner. Should be a good one. I'm not feeling tired or anything yet. I'm eating good and taking all the supplements Doc gave me. Still scared, I guess; maybe I'll be a little less scared since talking to you about this truth I'm supposed to be telling. But mostly I want to finish the season healthy and see if I can end this right. Really scared for my mom. Maybe even more for my dad. Cody. Man, I love him. It's always felt bad not telling but I just don't want all the complication. I want normal."

Hey-Soos puts a hand on my knee and again I feel it physically. "Slow down. You might want to consider that, relative to other people's lives, it's not *normal. I'm not sure it helps to pretend otherwise."*

And I pop awake.

I stand, walk to the window, gaze at a moonless, star-filled night, hoping for a cosmic answer I know isn't coming (as if I didn't just get one from Hey-Soos). So I go downstairs to the kitchen for a sandwich, which *will* come. *Whew.* I've been counting on the fact that I made a good decision to keep what was happening to myself, and not burden other people so I didn't have to burden myself with their responses. That was the one no-brainer back in the summer and it was wrong. Shit. I don't know what to do for sure, but no matter what, I'm not telling until football season is over because they'd snatch me out of my pads so fast the pads would still be standing, so I have either one or two weeks to think about it, depending on what happens with Timberline.

Thirteen

Timberline High School, which includes the towns Pierce and Weippe from up north, has had the same season we've had. They're overloaded in the talent department, just like we are—*were* before we lost Sooner Cowans—and came through the season undefeated with only a couple of close games. Their one-two punch comes in the form of the Brown brothers, Timothy and Shoat, identical-twin full-blooded Nez Percé Indians, who, as anyone who has played them will tell you, are virtually interchangeable. They're not that big, a little under six feet and maybe a hundred sixty pounds, but they're fast and wily and they switch positions on demand. It's crazy watching the films. They're numbers 6 and 7, and until they line up you never know which will line up at QB and which will line up at receiver. And you don't have to watch for long to think they have the telepathy thing going.

The game is billed by the Boise newspaper as the *actual* state championship. The teams from the southern part of the state don't have the talent pool, so the real state championship game will likely be a blowout, though Coach will tell you on any given Friday afternoon, anything can happen.

We're playing at Boise State. There is all kinds of hype because Cody will likely go there and because identical-twin Native American brothers make great press. Timothy and Shoat won't be matriculating to a college; they're both already promised to the United States government for at least four years. They're headed for a way different kind of war.

We get out of school on Wednesday and go down to stay in a hotel near the college so we can get used to the field. Timberline does the same. None of us has ever played on artificial turf and to make it even more surreal, Boise State has the only deep blue artificial turf in the nation. You walk onto the field and think you're playing the Smurfs. Eight jillion screaming Catholics at Notre Dame aside, it may be the biggest home court advantage in the country.

We have different practice times, so we're not on the field with Timberline, but we get a chance to watch them from the bleachers and they see us, also.

It's hard to tell if the blue turf creates an illusion or if we're in for a real horse race, because these guys look *fast*. They aren't particularly big, but hey, no eight-man team is, and they're coached like we are. Cody and I stand in the bleachers watching them work special teams. These guys are serious.

"We'll stay up late tonight," Cody says on the short bus ride back to the hotel. "Go over the tapes until I see 'em in my sleep. Get a good night's sleep tomorrow and give these guys a shock. Man, we could sure use Cowans."

Cody couldn't be more right. One guy makes a much greater difference in eight-man football than in eleven. It's like Arena Ball on a full-size field. One guy getting consistently beat on defense will kill you; same with not being able to spring a guy loose on offense. Cowans may not have the brightest future after high school, but he doesn't feel pain and he can run and catch with the best of them and we're going to miss the extra dimension he gives us. So this will be Cody's show. If he pulls it off, Boise State will have to give him a shot. If he has a game anywhere close to as good as his Horseshoe Bend game, the BSU scouts will go nuts. And Boise, Idaho, is fucking crazy about football. I mean, they have a *blue* football field.

Game Day

Boise has a full-size stadium that they pack with every college game, and though our two small towns don't fill it to capacity, they don't lack for excitement. The atmosphere is electric. The bands take turns on the blue turf with their pregame performances; cheerleaders cartwheel and dance to the music and challenge one another to create hearing loss. I don't know that I've felt anything like this.

In a shot at a psychological boost, Coach makes his first tactical error of the year. He sends Sooner out with my brother to meet the captains of Timberline: the brothers Brown, whose silky black hair falls to their shoulder pads. My brother reaches across and shakes their hands but Sooner raises one hand as if he's being sworn in in a courtroom, and my brother backhands him hard in the chest. The brothers nod and walk away. When Cody gets close to the huddle, I ask what Sooner did.

"Fucker said, 'How, Chief.'"

Coach was busy giving the rest of us instructions so he missed it; he pulls us in tight. "This is it, guys. Everybody expects both teams to have the jitters for the first few plays, but don't let that happen. I don't want to try to come from behind on these guys. Do what you've done all year. The field's a hundred yards long and the crossbar on the goalpost is ten feet high. The only difference is Smurf Turf and more people in the stands; those things are equal for both teams. Play smart and play hard. We've busted our butts to get here, now let's get one more." We line up to kick off.

I have a feeling it's a bad idea to introduce yourself to either of the Brown brothers like a movie star cowboy, because Shoat takes the opening kickoff eighty-seven yards across our goal line and he is untouched. Then he jogs over to our sideline and hands Sooner the ball and jogs back to midfield to get ready for *their* kickoff. Cody comes over and slaps Sooner on the ass and says, "Way to go, big guy," and is back onto the field before Sooner can tell him to fuck himself.

Cody doesn't find his rhythm and we're three downs and out. Timberline scores another touchdown before we can solve our Native American problem, then Cody catches fire. Through the rest of the half he fires one score to me and one to Dolven on a guard eligible, but Timberline answers each time and we're playing two touchdowns behind. Our crowd never gives up and theirs is off the charts, and the bands battle each other almost as hard as we're battling on the field. Though Cody has a brilliant game at quarterback with over three hundred yards passing and running and I get my share of catches and tackles, we never get within one touchdown. Nobody gives up and the crowd gets to see a hell of a football game, but the rocket ride Timberline gets from Sooner's slight is too big to make up and our season is over.

Sitting on the bench in my soaked T-shirt and jock in the Boise State locker room, I want to blame Sooner. He's walking around slapping guys on the back, telling them they played great but maybe we needed him out there. I'm thinking we had him out there too much, and I'm *this* close to walking over and telling him to shut the fuck up and taking the hit.

Cody sits beside me. "You were great, little big bro," he says, watching Sooner make his rounds. He shakes his head. "A thinking man's sport." He looks up to see a scout from BSU standing near the door and slaps me on the knee. "Be back."

The scout smiles and extends his hand and I know they're going to offer Cody something, and I relax a little. That's what I wanted most. But even through my paralyzing fatigue a thought drifts through. Football was my insulation; the thing I had put between me and dying. I wanted to replicate the Horseshoe Bend game today. I wanted that one more catch and I wanted that one more game. For me and for Coach.

But I had my season. It was more than I could have asked for. Thanks to Sooner's old man I didn't take anyone's spot or cost anyone a chance to be a hero, and I got to see what it felt like. I am hugely appreciative, even if it didn't turn out exactly like I wanted.

Sunday afternoon I head down to Trout Auto to make a few bucks washing and waxing some showroom cars, and to catch up with Rudy. The Halls don't open Sundays, so I won't have to listen to what all we could have done to win the game. They both played here, too.

"So," Rudy says, "season's over, huh?"

"Yup," I say. "Not a bad one."

"Not bad for you because you didn't get killed."

"Yeah. Let's talk about something else."

He holds his copy of *The Autobiography of Malcolm X.* "You finish it?"

"I did. It's like you said, old Malcolm covers a lot of spiritual distance. Ended like I remembered, though. He still gets killed for trying to stop the hate."

"He gets killed for threatening a power structure," Rudy says.

"And he went to the most dangerous part of the world today to find his peace. It's like proof you can find meaning anywhere."

Rudy just nods. He looks slightly pained.

"Threatening a power structure. Is that what you did? With the church?"

"In a way," Rudy says. "It's more complicated than that." He sounds like he wants to talk about that about as much as I wanted to talk about the game.

This is the place in a classroom discussion where the teacher usually tells me to shut the hell up, but every direction I look, there's more I don't know and I have so little *time.*

"More complicated how?"

"Some other time," Rudy says. "For now, let's stick to Malcolm. This much will give you all the ammo you need for your civics teacher."

I take a deep breath. "Okay. Malcolm."

"High school and college for me were the sixties," Rudy says. "Civil rights was hot. Freedom Riders were driving from north to south to help; most of them without a clue how to do that. A few of 'em got killed. Martin Luther King Jr. was struggling because a new brand of black person was emerging, fed up with eating shit, a brand that believed it had nothing to lose by fighting back.

"I was unaware of all that. I grew up in a town like this one, only in the Midwest. Mostly white, like this. We didn't notice our racial issues because we barely had any races. Malcolm came and went, barely blipping my radar. I remember being glad it was black guys who shot him because then they couldn't blame us. I may have thought he got what he deserved. Came out this direction to Gonzaga for my undergraduate work. Already knew I was headed for the priesthood."

"You were eighteen and wanted to be a priest? Did you know what that *meant*?"

"You mean no girls? Yeah, I knew what it meant. I had my reasons. At any rate GU wasn't a lot more diverse than my hometown and nothing in me changed, though the country was going through major turmoil with the war in Vietnam and all the racial unrest. Poor people were doing most of the fighting even though there was a draft; there were a million ways out if you had money . . . but I wasn't paying attention to that. I was focused on my own demons. I wanted to be a priest."

Whew.

"And then I was, and it wasn't what I expected and I started looking for some real truths. I read Malcolm's book, or Haley's book on Malcolm, and then I read up on Cesar Chavez and King and Gandhi, and a hundred other men and women on the front lines trying to make the world livable and I realized I was being left behind. But I was scared to leave and I started trying to work from within, and then . . . "

Rudy looks almost dreamy, then a pained look comes across his face and he snaps out of it. I fold my polishing rag and sit in the folding chair next to him. He reaches across and squeezes my knee, looks me right in the eye. "Things spun out of control. Ben, never let things spin out of control. It's too hard to get it back."

"You mean . . . "

He lets go of my knee and sits back. "Enough for today. That book was simply the one that got me fired up. Any good book can do it."

● ● ●

I'm lying facedown on Dallas Suzuki's couch while she straddles me, massaging my back and shoulders. It feels so good I'm considering paying her the money I earned cleaning cars. Her mom is in her bedroom and we have put Joe Henry to bed. "I might have to do another article on you, little man," she says. "You had quite a season."

"You didn't have a bad one yourself. I was lucky enough to be with more talented players."

She kneads along the sides of my spine.

"Mmmmmmmmmmmmm." This is deep tissue work; maybe not as good as sex, but it will stand in nicely until sex comes along. "Sooo good," I say. "A little higher on the shoulders. Oh gawwwd! Will you marry me? We don't have to live together or anything. I'll just come over once a week. You don't even have to talk to me."

I can feel her smiling. She massages a few more minutes in silence, then, "Do you think we have a chance?"

"At what?"

"Being together."

I'm quiet a second, my mind racing. If she means *now.* "Sure."

"You're not just in it for . . . "

"The sex? What sex?"

She slaps my back. "The future sex."

"Dallas, I gotta tell you . . . I really like you. I mean, I *really* like you."

"Can you prove that in a court of law?"

"I can prove it anywhere."

"Is your love for me unconditional?" she says.

"Unconditional."

"What if I got in a horrible car wreck and my face was disfigured. . . . "

"I'm your guy," I say.

"And lost my arms and legs . . . "

I wince, which she can't see. None of this is likely; I won't have to prove it. "Still your guy."

"Would you love me if I were a man?"

"No!"

"You said it was unconditional."

"Yeah, but . . . "

She slaps my back. "How am I ever going to trust you?"

"Would you love me if I were a twelve-foot python?" I say.

"Twice as much," she says back.

"With oozing reptilian sores?"

"Four times as much."

"Hmmm."

"I think women are just superior beings," she says. "Maybe I'll have to make do."

We're quiet and she starts rubbing my back again. "How about this?" she says after a few seconds. "Would you love me if Joe Henry were my little boy instead of my brother?"

Different tone. "What?"

"He's my son," she says.

Her hands rest on my shoulders.

I do the math in my head.

"Thirteen," she says. "Barely."

"Wow. Your uncle?"

"Right. So how fast do you want to run for your pickup?"

"I'm not running for my pickup." I have *no* idea what this means.

So she tells me. "As soon as we graduate I'm coming out with it." Her voice quivers ever so slightly. "It's been awful. When I first told my mother about Uncle Roy she slapped my face, and then I got pregnant and she couldn't deny it. She is big-time Catholic so there was no getting rid of it, which I wanted to do and am *really* glad

I didn't. Since then it's just been this monstrous secret. That's why you don't see her around much; she thinks you already know. Anyway, once we went through all the sleight of hand—Mom told everyone she was pregnant and we were going to live with the father, then came back after Joe Henry was born and said the dad abandoned us—I couldn't make myself tell the truth. But I'm going to because it's been like carrying a hot coal right here in my chest," and I hear her knuckle knock against her breastbone, "and Mom can just figure out what she's going to say. I mean, Joe Henry and I are off to college, so I won't have to stay around and listen to it, but Mom's on her own because I'm full up, and you're the only person in the world that knows this and I need to know if you're going to stay or run."

Wow.

She sits up, and so do I, wrapping my arm around her shoulder.

I say, "Stay."

"I hate secrets," she says, and though her voice is strong, tears stream down her cheeks. "They'll kill you. They're worse than my uncle." She turns to me. "I don't want you to make any commitment or marry me or any of that. We don't even have to go to the same college. I just need to know nothing changes now that you know."

And the stakes go up. Because I *would* be around. Joe Henry is the coolest little shit in the universe and I already like helping to train him to grow up to be hard to deal with. But I ain't gonna be around nothin' for long, and I'm a coward and I miss my chance. "I'll be around," I say, "unless I get hit by a truck or something."

"If you were going to die, you'd have been killed playing football," she says, wiping her eyes.

Shit.

Fourteen

On Thanksgiving, Dad and Cody and I sit on the couch around the coffee table eating holiday nuts and watching the Dallas Cowboys get their heads handed to them. The bad news is the nuts are probably dinner. Mom's locked in her room and Dad has the cooking skills of a dirt clod. The good news is Christmas will be better; her down time seldom lasts a full month. Shortly after halftime I answer the doorbell to find Coach on the porch.

"Hey, Coach. What's up?"

"What's up?" he says. "Dinner's up. You guys invited me, right?"

I'm thinking Dad or Cody screwed up in a big way, 'cause Coach isn't even toting a bottle of wine for him and Dad.

"Uh . . ."

He whacks the side of my head. "I'm messing with you, Wolfman," and turns for his car. "Come on. Give me a hand."

I stare into the back of his SUV, which smells like a four-star restaurant—like I'd know what a four-star restaurant smells like. Coach has prepared an entire Thanksgiving dinner: cranberry sauce, marshmallow-covered yams, and all. He must have turned into Emeril. "Let's get 'er in there while she's still hot," he says and picks up the turkey roaster. Within minutes we're sitting around the table like a regular family with two dads. Dad and Coach are cordial, but you sense them avoiding the gorilla in the kitchen, my mother's closed door. I think my dad is embarrassed for someone on the outside to see this part of our family secret, but he knows Coach has seen it before and it's safe with him. I don't know that they've ever discussed it. Coach is respectful of Dad's embarrassment and also of Dad's inability to change it. The most intimate thing said during the entire time is, "How 'bout them Cowboys."

Early December
"So Thanksgiving is behind us, the football season has drawn to a merciful close, and we're all equal again,"

Lambeer says to start class. Mr. Lambeer believes athletes, particularly male athletes, and more particularly football players, get a free ride around here, which we do, but not for any fault of the coaches. Coach Banks has seniority and most coaches follow his philosophy of jocks being simply guys who play games and who shouldn't get special privileges. It's just that when you're winning, Mac Sebring and Luke Bryson, who run Trout's two restaurants, tend to give you two burgers for the price of one and Rich Graham, who runs Trout Sports and Small Engine, is likely to give you a stunningly low price on T-shirts that sport his logo. Those guys are throwbacks, so female athletes aren't held in the same high regard.

"That final game was a good one, guys. Very enjoyable even though the result wasn't exactly what we might have hoped for." It's hard to tell if he's totally serious or if sarcasm is creeping in, but it doesn't matter; the season is over and the hoopsters start tonight and soon it will be all about putting the round ball through the round hole, which Cody and Dallas excel at and I don't. They're both closer to the hole. So they will stay in the limelight and I'll figure out what to do with the rest of the year or the rest of my life, whichever comes first.

I've been freaked out since my conversation with Dallas the other night. I watch her from two rows over this morning and she looks as normal as anything. She and the other lady hoopsters were in the cafeteria this morning talking up the season, and as I stood in the entrance watching it almost seemed as if our conversation never happened. But it did and I sat right there and lied to her. I tried to convince myself it wasn't a lie *really*, as in technically, but if you think about it, any time you want someone to think something different than what is true, it's a lie.

Little things keep popping up in my head, like does Joe Henry know? I've never heard him call her Momma or Mommy. In fact he calls her Dallas Suzuki. Little screwball uses her whole name. And who played the mom role back when he was a baby and she was thirteen? And what was it like to be dragged off by your mom to have that baby when Uncle Roy was still on the loose? What did they tell the doctors? I know if a doctor hears that, he or she has to report it. Even if they went several states away, somebody would have showed up to pluck Uncle Roy out of his house and the truth would have leaked out. And God, she had to *have* it. Thirteen. It's supposed to hurt like crazy to have a baby. I didn't ask any of those questions Friday night. I just said I'd stay.

"Ben?" Lambeer says. "You with us?"

"Right here," I say.

"Well?"

"I'm right here now, but I just got here. What was the question?"

"We talked last week about your changing your project. Have you rethought that, given the time you have?"

"Yes I've rethought it, and no I decided not to change it," I say. "I'm bringing Malcolm X into current events. I'm starting a grassroots campaign to have a street here in Trout named after him."

I hear that I have tickled my classmates.

Sooner says low, from the seat behind me, "Shit, Wolf, what's the matter with you? We're not namin' no street after a—"

"Uh, as has been mentioned," Lambeer says, "you live in a town of zero percent African-American inhabitants. Even if I were to change my mind and let you do it, where would you get your signatures?"

"I'll start with anyone who was around for the sixties," I say. "That's how a grassroots campaign takes root."

"Well, I'm *not* going to change my mind, so it's moot."

"It's moot, except I'm doing it anyway."

Sylvia Longley, of book-burning fame, says, "Stand up for this, Mr. Lambeer. Somebody in this school needs to have some sense."

Lambeer looks pleased. "I fully intend to stand up for it. Ben, do you realize that if you receive a failing grade on this project you could receive a failing grade for the course, costing you your diploma?"

"I'm realizing it just this minute," I say.

"And you're willing to do that. You have probably a three-point-seven grade average, are looking at a bright future, and you'd sacrifice it all to make this point?"

"Naw," I say. "I'd really only be sacrificing three months. I could take the course in summer school down in Boise or somewhere and hit the ground running in the fall."

Dallas says, "This Wolf kid is smarter than he looks."

Randy Dolven says, "He'd have to be." Dolven's comment isn't mean-spirited. He disses everyone. Sooner, on the other hand, would move out of a town before allowing a street to be named after a black guy. I think I'll campaign to make it his street.

"I have decided, after reading *Lies My Teacher Told Me*—I love that title by the way—that we're still an inherently bigoted country. Our history books are whitewashed of our racial history, particularly recent racial history. Did you know back then the director of the FBI actually undertook a smear campaign on Martin Luther King, Jr.? But I digress. This project is particularly current because Malcolm X learned acceptance after going to *Mecca,* which, like I said before, is right in the middle of all the nastiness today. It's like ironic, or whatever. And there will be a lesson if I'm successful and a lesson if I'm not. We'll all learn something."

"We may have our racial problems, but the United States of America is the freest country in the world, for *every* race. On what do you base your assumptions of racism?"

"Living here," I say. "Watching old news clips from New Orleans when Hurricane Katrina hit and then watching the Spike Lee HBO movie. Did you know they found dead bodies more than a year after Hurricane Katrina? No way that happens in, like, Beverly Hills, California. When the World Trade Center was bombed they *combed* through the rubble. It's all we heard about. The President was at *that* site within days. We might not still have lynchings, but that doesn't mean bigotry is gone."

"I picked up Loewen's book since the last time you

mentioned it," Lambeer says, "and I hate to tell you it is *decidedly* left leaning."

"Perfect," I say. "If I read it *and* our textbook and listen to you, I should land exactly in the middle. And if only half of what in there is true, we still have problems with racism."

"Plus, Katrina was a while ago," Lambeer says, "and there are other circumstances that went with that. I don't think you can call it racism or bigotry."

"Well, then," I say, "what do you call Sooner Cowans walking out to the coin toss at the Timberline game and saying "How" while he raised his hand like some two-bit movie star cowboy?"

Sooner is up like a flash. "That there was a joke, you little punk," he says. "I didn't know the brothers Injun was gonna take offense."

"Did you keep the ball they gave you?" I say, turning toward him. He's coming but so is Cody; I'm safe. I turn back to Lambeer. "I rest my case."

Lambeer says, "I don't think Mr. Cowans meant to be racist. I'll admit if that happened it was a bit insensitive. . . . "

"That's how racism works," I say back. "You should read *Malcolm X*." Sooner is stopped in his tracks, as is my brother, standing fast waiting for him to sit back down. "That's how any bigotry works."

Sooner says, "You better watch your mouth, midget."

"Careful, Cowans," I tell him. "You might piss off some midgets."

"You make a case, Mr. Wolf, even though it's a flawed one," Lambeer says. "I guess I'm not willing to let you throw your diploma away on stubbornness, so I'll let you do the project. But I'll cut it off in a heartbeat if I hear anything negative from the townspeople. Sooner, sit down."

My brother hasn't said a word. He's leaning against Nessa Milner's desktop, just keepin' the peace. Nessa Milner doesn't seem to mind.

Dallas raises her hand. "Mr. Lambeer, what would you say if I told you I thought I should never have to pay taxes to the United States Government?"

"I'd say you had better plan to spend a good deal of your life behind bars, Ms. Suzuki. Why do you ask?"

"Did you know that during World War Two my grandparents were given one day to get everything they could carry, then sent to a concentration camp in Arkansas?"

"Those were called relocation centers, Ms. Suzuki. Not concentration camps."

"I know what the government called them, Mr. Lambeer," and she says his title with the same pomposity he uses for hers, "and I learned right in this room that nuclear warheads are called Peacemakers and the relaxation of pollution restrictions is called the Clean Air Act. They were concentration camps."

Whoa! Dallas is using weapons she gathered right in this room to make a point I think Lambeer's not going to like. Maybe I *would* love her even if she were a man.

"And your point is . . . "

"That my father got cheated out of a substantial inheritance, which probably cost him a college education and a job that would have allowed him to at least pay his child support, which I might use to go to college. My grandparents or my father or my uncle never received a penny in reparations. And if you're African-American or Native American, well, where should I start? We don't even admit our historical racism. How would you expect us to recognize current racism? I think we could all learn a lot from the responses Ben gets doing his project."

"First, Ms. Suzuki, I could take issue with your characterization of the relocation camps as racist. We were, after all, at war with the Japanese."

"My grandparents never set foot in Japan. All their *l*s and *rs* were in place."

"As I said, I'm allowing Mr. Wolf to go ahead with his project, as long as it doesn't cause too much trouble."

To some degree, the idea of lobbying for Malcolm X Avenue was a joke, because I knew how far it would get up Lambeer's nose and because I could have some fun learning local political process at the same time. I mean, I certainly don't expect the good people of Trout, Idaho, to name a street after a street criminal turned activist turned wise man turned dead guy. But when Dallas was laying it on Lambeer this afternoon, there was *passion* behind her words. If I do this right, I can fuck with Lambeer and be Dallas Suzuki's hero at the same time. It might get better than that, but not on this planet.

Truth is, I use the Malcolm X factor as an excuse to see Rudy. I know all I need to know without the up close and personal history. But Rudy seems interested and it gets me into the garage, where I can kind of keep an eye on him. He didn't have any effect on me at all until I came into my own dire straits, but here's a guy everyone thinks is a throwaway, on the downhill slide of his life; a decent guy with a good mind who could exit so quietly no one but the Hall brothers would know he was gone. Doesn't seem right.

But when I get to the garage Rudy is seriously shit-faced. I mean *embalmed.* It's like he's been drinking steady since I last saw him, and he is not cordial. I've got my copy of *Malcolm X* in hand and underlined and he tries to rip it out of my hands, after I finally scream at him loud enough for him to let me in.

"Gimme that goddam book!" he bellows. "Gimme that goddam thing!"

"Rudy, what the hell?" I'm holding the book out of his reach, though I don't have to worry about him actually getting it. He has to be seeing at least three. "What happened? You were *clean.*"

"And fuckin' sober," he says. "Clean an' fuckin' sober. Tell you what, that ain't all i's cracked up to be. I don' wan' you comin' round here no more. No more supplements, you hear? You stay away."

"What?"

"You heard me. You wash your goddam cars durin'

the day and stay the hell away at night. I got work to do. I can't be spendin' my time on a buncha books that don' mean shit. They're ancient hishtory."

I don't have time for this. I walk over to the workbench and wrap my fingers around an almost drained bottle of Jack Daniels and sling it across the room where it *pops* like a rifle shot. Then I go to the drawers where he used to keep his stash to find out what he has left. I yell "Bullshit!" each time I fling one. Six bottles: six bullshits. Rudy is screaming at me, calling me every name in the book, trying to get to me, but I'm dancing around the room ahead of him, firing those babies at the wall and letting him know that next time I come down here to save his drunken ass, he'd better be ready to have it saved. By the time I'm finished he's on the floor crying like a baby, begging me to stop, which is where he passes out.

Rudy's a pretty good-sized guy and I'm not what you'd call a heavy lifter, but I get him across the room to his cot, head on the pillow, boots off, and cover him with his blanket. I won't stay all night, but I'll get back before he can get to the liquor store, and before business hours, and get this shit unraveled.

● ● ●

Fucking Rudy. I'm exhausted. At home my mother's bedroom door is closed, and Dad is asleep on the couch. The drapes are wide open and a full moon pours light through the picture window, casting the room in a kind of blue calm. It's a fake calm, though. I sit in Dad's easy chair, staring at his chest moving up and down easily in sleep. Once in a while, if he thinks Mom might pull out of it, he sleeps here so he can hear her. Fucking Rudy. I want to walk over to my mother's room and kick the door in and jerk her out of that stupid bed and tell her to get her shit together. Man, I wish I'd never told Marla I was dying. Then I'd still have a therapist and maybe I could find out where in hell I ever got the idea I had to save every unsavable wretch I come across, starting with my mother and ending with fucking Rudy. In a couple of days, just to keep Doc Wagner at arm's length, I've agreed to go see the new therapist, some guy named Alex Wells, who has taken over for Marla. It would be nice if he's a good one.

I lie back in the chair and stare at the moon and try to get my heart rate down, then look over at Dad again, wondering if there was ever a time when he felt about my mother the way I do about Dallas. I drift off, hoping he did.

● ● ●

"So much for Rudy McCoy."

"You mean because he's in the bag again?"

"Yeah," I say. *"Way in the bag."*

"You might want to be a little more patient. Things aren't always as they seem. The universe works in strange and mysterious ways."

"So I've heard. Actually, I always thought the strange and mysterious ways argument was just a cop-out."

"The way most people interpret it, it is. All it really means is there's a lot in the universe that humans don't understand. But the truth doesn't need to be known, or believed, to be true."

Add *that* line to the evidence that Hey-Soos and I are not one and the same.

"Don't worry about it," Hey-Soos says before I can once again bring his origins into question.

"What do you think about my Malcolm X Avenue idea?"

"Do you know who Don Quixote is?"

I say I do.

"Then I think it's a great idea. I'm behind you all the way, but just so you know what I think your chances are, I won't plug that street into my GPS system."

I don't bother to ask him why a guy with his seeming connections would need a GPS system. "One more thing."

"Shoot."

"Is there any way around telling people what's happening to me? Like Dallas and my brother at least?"

"Go back and remember why you made that decision in the first place."

"I already told you. I did it because I want to live a normal life."

"And I said . . . "

"'You're dying. What's normal about that?'"

He raises his holy eyebrows. "If you don't want to take my word for it, maybe you should take it up with your new counselor."

Fifteen

In the morning I let myself into the Halls Garage about six-thirty, which is pretty easy because I left the door unlocked when I dragged Rudy to bed last night. I'm expecting him to be an asshole of the highest degree, but I played a full football season with Sooner Cowans and I'm still ambulatory, so it takes a lot to scare me.

He is in the exact same position I left him and if his snoring didn't sound like he's clear-cutting the last stand of yellow pine in the county, I might think he's dead. What the hell, I shake him. He grunts and turns over so I shake him again. He waves his arms as if I'm a giant mosquito and says something very unpriestlike. I shake him again.

He looks at me, through me, really, then I see in his eyes what I can only describe as terror. He shoves me away and sits up.

"Jesus, Rudy. What's the *matter* with you?"

He stands and staggers a few steps across the greasy concrete floor, runs his hands over his face. "You can't come here anymore."

"I work here. I can come any time I want."

"You need to stay away from me," he says. "It was a mistake to get sober. A bigger one to start talking to you."

"Hey, what'd I do?"

"Will you just get out of here?"

"No!"

He glares at me for a long moment, then sighs. "I guess this is the only way." There is this . . . *desperation* in his eyes. "Sit down."

I sit.

He takes a deep breath. "I'm a child molester," he says, at which time I stop breathing.

He leans his elbows on the workbench, drops his face into his hands. "That's why I joined the priesthood."

"So you could get to kids?" My mind is spinning.

"Jesus, no. So I'd stay away from kids. I was . . . You sure you want to hear this?"

I'm not, but I say I am.

"If I'm going to tell this I have to tell it all. I can't have you running out of here before I get it said."

I want to run out *now*, but I'm as fascinated as I am repulsed. I see Dallas and her uncle. I don't see them really; I've never seen her uncle, but you know what I mean. "Go ahead."

"I was in my twenties when I realized I was fascinated with young boys. I tried everything to make it not true: drank, used drugs, went out with as many pretty girls as would go out with me. Only every time I tried to have sex, it . . . it just didn't work, and I was thinking about kids. Boys.

"I made a couple of lame suicide attempts, none of which could have killed me, then I found myself hanging around schools and parks. Scary stuff. I grew up Catholic so I started going to church every Sunday, sitting in the empty church for hours at a time on weeknights, praying to God to help me. And I thought He did. I walked out of the church late one night, knowing my only escape was to give myself over to Him. I pledged to enroll in seminary and become a priest. I figured if I stayed as close to God as I could, He'd keep me safe."

I've read way too many newspapers to think this is going to turn out well, but I am speechless. I have this awful feeling in the back of my throat, and yet, he's *Rudy*. I mean, I'm not scared of Rudy.

"Only God was nowhere to be found. Kids were there." He shakes his head slowly as his voice cracks. "Sometimes I wonder if I lied to myself, did it on purpose, like you said, to get closer to them. I was an altar boy once, though nothing happened to me."

"You were never molested?" I've heard that most molesters usually were molested as kids.

"I was molested, but not in the church. In fact it was my priest who got me help. That's another story. I'll tell you that one if you survive this one. At any rate, things were fine for a long time. I was ordained and eventually placed in a small diocese in northern Michigan, pretty close to where I grew up. I did everything by the book. The town loved me. I had fantasies, of course, but I said them out loud to God and every day I asked Him to watch over me. And it seemed as if He did. "Keep telling me," He said, "and I'll keep you safe."

Rudy looks toward the corner of the ceiling, but *way* past the corner if you see his eyes. Way past and back in time. "Then there was Donny Blankenship. Great kid.

Good little athlete. His parents brought him to me when he was eleven because they wanted him to experience being an altar boy, like his father. The Blankenships were my friends. They had me to dinner; I played golf with them. I was almost a part of their family." Rudy seems to be talking to himself now, barely aware I'm here.

"The moment they brought him to me, I was aware of the attraction. I should have said no, made some excuse, but I brought him in. Classic grooming. I prayed and prayed. God kept telling me it was okay, that I had thoughts but it was my behavior that counted. Keep praying and don't worry. Only it wasn't God talking at all. It was Rudy McCoy, setting, baiting the trap. I groomed Danny and I groomed myself.

"And then one day he came to see me in my office, completely down. His girlfriend had chosen someone else, and he was devastated. Thirteen years old. First girlfriend. He needed comfort and I gave it to him, and I gave him more. He was confused and I told him all the right lies, how he was special, maybe it was a good thing his girlfriend had left, and how God wanted him to help a good priest find his way; that the church expected special things from special people. My God, I was making it up as I went, and he was vulnerable and young and confused and scared. The perfect victim."

I can't articulate the repulsion I feel. I can see this kid, feel him. He's me trying to take care of Mom, trying to please her just to be the person who gives her that feeling she never gets. It's me wishing I could make my father feel better, give him something to live for that is for him and not for my broken mother or us. I see Donny Blankenship like he's in the room.

"And it went on and on and I hated myself and told myself I would stop and that I would find a way to make it up to him, but he just got quieter and more compliant. I went to his family's home for holidays, continued to play golf with his father. I sat in his living room, separating myself further and further from the truth. All the signs were there. His parents came to me, said his grades were dropping, he was losing interest in sports.

"My God, I counseled him for more than a year as if nothing was going on. And he accepted my counseling. And then I was walking past the pews *very* early one morning and found him, slumped to the side, a bullet through his head, all evidence of his life drained out in the blood soaking into the wood. I missed him by maybe a half hour." Rudy's eyes well with tears. "I murdered a fourteen-year-old boy."

I said I'd stay through this, but I want to run. I just want to run. I can barely breathe.

He takes a deep breath. "I covered my ass. At his parents' request I presided over the funeral. His father, who was a pretty tough nut, told me again and again in the back room after the service how grateful he was that his son had me to talk to; he realized how emotionally unavailable he had been. He blamed himself, and I kept quiet.

"As soon as the church was empty, I got a bottle and started drinking. About midnight, I burned all my vestments in the woodstove in the small dwelling the church provided, got into my car, and started driving. Over the next few months I discovered that, through heavy doses of painkillers I'd been prescribed for a back injury and alcohol, I could blunt my desires. I've stayed drunk and fucked up ever since.

"I happened to be here in Trout when my car broke down and the Halls took me in to keep me from freezing. I've hid here since. Every day I wake up and hate myself and until I fell in with your great experiment of health and supplements, I medicated myself." He nods and lets out a deep breath, looks away. "That's my story and I'm sticking to it."

I'm numb. "Why are you telling me now?"

He hangs his head. I wait. "Because I told myself that if I ever got even close to that position again, I'm outta here." He looks at me.

"Me?"

"I think it's because you're small," Rudy says. He snorts, a snort brimming over with self-contempt. "You're actually too old for me. I–"

I stand. "Look, I gotta go."

He smiles. He looks tired. Not sleepy. Life tired.

"Listen," he says.

I put up my hands. "I gotta go, Rudy. I just . . . I gotta go." And I'm gone.

I am in my pickup with the key in the ignition and the transmission in reverse and my foot on the gas in less time than it takes a NASCAR guy to make a pit stop, and I am driving down Main Street. What the hell is going on in my short life? I've been on a comet since Doc Wagner delivered my news. The universe has handed me things I'd have never dared to want. Dallas Suzuki. The mantle of a football hero. Monstrous esteem. Yet it's taking the one thing I took for granted: my life. And now it's showing me subtleties, paradoxes, almost no one gets to see. And those subtleties are fucking with my fundamental understanding of right and wrong, which I've got to get down in a hurry because I don't have time not to.

The two days before my appointment with my new therapist can't pass fast enough. But then:

"So you're Ben Wolf."

"Yes sir."

"Ben, I'm Dr. Wells."

"It says on your door that you're Mr. Wells, M.A. That's not a doctor." I don't know why I'm being a smart-ass. I think I'm still mad I lost Marla and this guy doesn't look like he's going to be a Marla.

He smiles. He's young, probably late twenties, handsome in a dorky kind of way. He wears a tweed jacket and there is a pipe on his desk. He looks like Lambeer would look if he'd joined this profession. "Just have to defend my thesis," he says. "I'm asking my patients to call me Doctor so I can get used to it."

"Done," I say. "Do you have a first name?"

"I do," he says, but he doesn't tell me what it is.

I sit while he looks over Marla's notes. His master's diploma from Stanford University is framed on the wall behind him next to what I assume is his family coat of arms. Other framed pictures dot his walls, all depicting different facets of his undergraduate and graduate days at Stanford. I wonder what a guy with all this educational ammo is doing in Trout, Idaho.

"I'm perplexed by what I read here, Ben."

"If it says what I think it says, I'm perplexed, too."

"What is it you think it says?"

"That I'm toast."

"That's not the part that perplexes me," he says. "What perplexes me is that you've chosen to forgo traditional treatment for your disease and that you've chosen to keep it from your loved ones."

I start to say I'm perplexed that he's perplexed, but decide I don't want to go down in the book of *Guinness World Records* for the most uses of that word in a dialogue between a midget and a dickwad.

"I'm not sure I can work with you under these conditions," he says.

I look around the room and say, "We could turn down the lights and turn up the heat."

"Excuse me?"

"Different conditions," I say.

I detect that little marble muscle on the side of his

jaw. When I used to see it on my dad I called it the "uh-oh muscle."

"The way you're handling this situation is foolish," he says. "It leaves you with no support and it also leaves you without a strategy to fight this disease. I'm afraid I might be compelled to bring in reinforcements."

"What kind of reinforcements?"

"Your parents. Possibly your school." He reads a little farther. "I'm also considering reporting this Marla person to state licensing. She should never have allowed you to follow this course of treatment."

"She didn't have a choice," I say. "I made the decision before I met her. And if you 'bring in reinforcements,' *you'll* be the one with the state licensing problems."

"Actually I'm not sure that's true, Ben. You see, if I deem that you are a danger to self or others, I'm required to report that. Not getting treatment for a terminal illness is a danger to self."

I go from zero to really pissed off in about a second. "Not getting treatment for a terminal illness is a decision," I say. "Tell you what, in about a minute I'm going to excuse myself to go to the bathroom and instead of going to the bathroom I will leave the building. When you figure out I'm not coming back you get that little Not Amenable to Treatment stamp out of your top drawer and bring it down on my file folder. If one person I don't tell finds out about me being sick, you're gonna be an almost doctor for a long time because I will call Stanford University and whoever gives you guys licenses to practice and then I'll tell Sooner Cowans you've been messing with his girlfriend. *I'm* the person who decides how I live my life."

"Unfortunately, Ben, we're not talking about *living* your life. Who's Sooner Cowans?"

I'm up with my hand on the doorknob. "This might not be the best match."

To his credit, Not Quite Dr. Wells has taken at least one class in Hostile Adolescent Small People. "Tell you what," he says. "I'll back off on any decision about who I do or don't talk to. Let's you and I meet one more time, at least, and I'll give you a little assignment. I want you to write down as many things as you can think of that you'd like to do or learn while you're still . . . here."

I nod in agreement, mostly because I just want the hell out of here, but also because, even through the fog, it sounds like kind of a neat idea.

● ● ●

"Man, why didn't you warn me?"

"About what?"

"All the stuff that's going on. Like Rudy McCoy's a drunk and then he's an expriest, then he's my social conscious guru, then he's a child molester. Jesus, which is it?"

"I told you to call me Hey-Soos, and it's all of them."

"Man, what am I supposed to do now? You know what I'm supposed to do, don't you? I'm supposed to turn him in. The stats on those guys say they don't do just one kid. Dallas's uncle is a child molester. What do you think she'd say if she knew I was friends with one?"

"What do you think she'd say?"

"I think she'd say, 'Choose.' That's what I'd say if I was her. I'd say, 'That bastard wrecked my life and I'm not hanging with anyone who hangs with those bastards.'"

Hey-Soos says, "'If I were she.'"

"What?"

"You said, 'If I was her.' That's incorrect English. It's 'If I were she.'"

If I had any remaining suspicion that Hey-Soos isn't really the deeper me, it disappears. The deeper I. Me. Like I'd know that.

"If I were she. Sheesh. I'd get laughed out of school for saying that."

"So what are you going to do?" he says.

"I'm going to ask for your advice and do what you say."

"That's brave."

I say, "I'd rather be smart than brave on this one."

"What if I say you'll have to figure this one out for yourself?"

"Then I'll know you're really just me and you don't know."

"Trying to flush me out, huh?"

"Whatever. I just need to know what to do. I don't have the luxury of making a mistake."

"Okay, let's go over it. Do you think Rudy McCoy is an immediate danger to anyone?"

"No."

"Why not?"

"Because I think he was telling the truth," I say. "I think he's been keeping himself under control by staying fucked up on drugs and alcohol. No reason to tell me that if it wasn't true." Anyway, I don't think he's a danger."

"Do you think he's in *danger*?"

I consider that. Shit. "Yes."

"Why?"

"He hates himself. He doesn't have any control over what caused the worst thing he ever did."

Hey-Soos says, "Okay, how about Dallas?"

"What about her?"

"Is she in danger?"

"No, but like I said, if I hang out with a child molester, I might be."

"So how are you going to solve this?"

"I thought that's what you were here for. I don't know who to consider."

"Why don't you consider yourself?

"Because," I say, "I'm not a child molester and I haven't been molested. There's nothing to consider."

"How about considering who you are? Your impact? How about doing the least harm?"

There is a vast calm in my dream. I feel myself breathe. "Got it."

Sixteen

THINGS I WANT TO KNOW BEFORE I DIE

- Is it true that the day after Patty Hearst was kidnapped by the Symbionese Liberation Army in the seventies, McDonald's came out with a new hamburger called the Hearstburger? And that when you opened the bun you found no patty?

- Is it also true that in 1960 a young author named Lee Harper wrote a national best seller about a man who imitates and taunts birds of prey, called *To Mock a Killing Bird*?

- Is there really such a thing as Restless Leg Syndrome?

- Who killed President Kennedy?
- Now that Pluto has been relegated to the status of "dwarf planet" should it be my favorite?
- Will you be able to fill my time slot with someone who can be fixed?

Actually I'm not this much of a smart-ass, but I think you and I don't make a good match. Your question was a good one, though, and I've actually given it some real thought. Sorry I was such a jerk. Not your fault.

The Diminutive WolfMan

There's a note on the bulletin board near the school entrance indicating I'm supposed to see Mr. Lambeer before his class today. I'm a little early because I had to deliver my list to Almost Doctor Wells and because I've been cruising Main Street since seven o'clock, thinking I should go into Halls Garage and talk with Rudy. But I ran the dialogue every possible way I could think of and couldn't get it right.

Even with the morning's extracurricular activities I get to school almost twenty-five minutes before class starts, and hunt down Mr. Lambeer in his room. He is working on lesson plans. Rumor has it his are finished for the year. The guy is tight.

"Mr. Wolf."

"Mr. Lambeer." I nod.

"Have a seat."

"No thanks, I already have one," I say and pat my butt. You have to get up pretty early in the late evening to stay ahead of me. But I do sit. It's okay to joke with Lambeer as long as you do what he says.

"I hate to keep flip-flopping but I'm afraid I'm going to have to put the kibosh on your Malcolm X project again and I don't want to use a lot of class time arguing with you about it. That's why I asked you in."

"Why the kibosh?"

"I talked with Ernie Graves, who's chairman of the school board, and I have to agree with him. With the school bond levy coming up, it just makes us look frivolous."

I say, "But it's not frivolous. The lesson is there no matter the outcome. I get enough signatures for a referendum on a Malcolm X Avenue and it gets voted up or down. If I can't get the signatures, it dies. And part of the project is a discussion of people's verbal responses."

Lambeer puts on his skeptical look. "Ben, you can't tell me you're not going to try and make the people of Trout look bigoted and uneducated."

"I'll ask everyone the exact same questions. I'll show them to you before I do."

"Knowing what answer you'll get."

"But if I know the answer I get, if I can predict that closely, that says something about the nature of how we see race, at least in this small part of the country."

"That's the end of it, Ben. It's not going to happen."

Lambeer is digging a hole he doesn't want to be in, and he doesn't even know he's got a shovel. I raise my hands in surrender.

"I'm glad you understand," he says. "Now get busy choosing your project, because you're already way behind."

"I'm on it," I say at the door.

Now I figure a teacher gets you alone to deliver bad news for one of two reasons. Either he doesn't want you to be embarrassed in public or he doesn't want to be embarrassed himself. Of all my teachers, going way back to kindergarten, Lambeer is head and shoulders above all others for not giving a shit whether a student is embarrassed, so I figure the guy he's protecting wears his very same undershorts. I don't want to let him off quite so easily.

Beware the short terminal guy with nothing to lose.

• • •

I raise my hand as class begins.

"Mr. Wolf. Please tell me this has something to do with what we discussed about your term project."

"This has something to do with what we discussed about my term project," I say.

"Hallelujah," he says.

"Hosanna," I say back. I have no idea what that means.

"Fill me in."

"I'm doing the Malcolm project anyway. I've been thinking—"

Lambeer's jaw clamps. "Never a good thing," he says through gritted teeth.

"How can I respect myself if I don't do the project I think I'll learn from most?"

Lambeer says, "Frankly I'm not interested in your self-respect in this case."

"Lemme *make* my case," I tell him. "You'd have to agree that nothing is more current in this society than bigotry, and the pearl of bigotry is racism," and before he has a chance to respond, "and Malcolm is the perfect example of a guy who *got* it. He starts out as a street thug and a pimp, because that's the kind of well-paying job a black guy in his time could get. He goes to prison, starts to educate himself, comes out, and joins a group founded itself on bigotry, the Black Muslims, a group that called all white men devils. But Malcolm X is smart and he goes to the source, which is Mecca, and he finds every color of person there is in that crowd headed for Mecca and if he's gonna hate some color he's gotta hate some of the people walking down that road beside him. So he comes back to say, 'Hey, we're doin' it wrong,' and he gets shot by people who hate, for preaching inclusion."

"THAT'S ENOUGH!"

Oops. We have ignition.

"I've been as nice as I know how to be about this! I've let you take up way too much valuable class time with this foolishness! I'd better not hear another word! Not one more word! You will change your project or you will fail this class."

"Yes sir," I say.

"Good! Now what's your project going to be?"

"Afraid I have to stick with Malcolm."

I finish the period in the library.

● ● ●

So here I sit in Mr. Phelps's office with Phelps and Lambeer, neither of whom knows he's totally outclassed because he's about to try to reason with a guy who has no use for a diploma.

"Mr. Lambeer tells me you've become somewhat incorrigible in his classroom, Ben—to the extent that your grade is in danger. And he tells me that, though you're aware a failing grade could cost you your diploma, you won't change your attitude."

I look right at him, as if I'm waiting for the rest.

"Well?"

"Other than the incorrigible part, he's right."

"Mr. Lambeer has told me about your proposed project," Phelps says, "and I have to agree, it's frivolous."

I shrug.

"Ben, let's don't end the year this way. I don't understand this at all. You've never been a problem. I know you boys have troubles at home. . . . "

I say, "You think I'm doing this because I have a crazy mother?"

"No, of course not. Certainly not."

"Look, Mr. Phelps. I'm doing it because I decided at the beginning of this year that I wanted the most out of my education. That sounds all cheesy and stupid, I know, but it's the truth. I think this project will do me more good than any others I can think of. I recognize that Mr. Lambeer runs the class and I realize he has the right to flunk me if I don't do what he says. I know what I'm getting into and I know the consequences. I'm not going crying to my dad if I flunk. This is a free country, it's a class about government of a free country, and I have the right to fail."

"Ben, that makes no sense whatsoever. I can't allow that."

Lambeer sits erect in his seat, doesn't change expression, doesn't say a word.

"You can't not allow it," I say back to Phelps. "Look, I'm going to do the project, I'm going to write it up, I'm going to hand it in, and I'm going to take the grade I get. I've been warned. I'm taking everyone off the hook." I stand.

Phelps looks at Lambeer and shrugs. Lambeer stares straight ahead.

"Is that everything?" I ask. "Can I go now?"

There's no answer so I do.

Man, if you haven't given yourself permission to fail a class you need for graduation, you haven't lived.

Seventeen

When Rudy lets me in after eleven in the evening, he seems broken. He's not been drinking, though, or at least not so you can tell.

I say, "Hey," and place a package of supplements on the workbench. He's not out of the others, but it seems like a "familiar" thing to do to let him know we're okay.

"What are you doing back here?"

I point to the sack. "Here to make you well."

"What I have doesn't get well. I was expecting the cops."

"No cops," I say.

"Why not?"

"Well, there's a statute of limitations on charging you, and besides I didn't tell anyone."

"You should have."

"Look, Rudy. What you did was seriously fucked up. I mean fucked *up*. But you obviously already know that or you wouldn't have spent the last however many years of your life drunk and lost in Podunk, Idaho. But man, you gotta convince me you haven't done it to anyone else. I mean, I looked on the internet. . . . "

"If I'd done it to anyone else, I wouldn't be here," he said. "I wouldn't be anywhere. I don't have much by way of redemption, but I have that."

I can't help it. Right or wrong, I believe him. "And you didn't try anything with me. You told me the truth. That took us both out of danger. I mean, hell, you're an old guy and I can outrun you. Besides that I'm a football hero."

You told me the truth.

I'm suddenly feeling even worse about hiding my own death penalty. I can't be my brother's best friend while hiding something that big. I can't expect to be loved by Dallas after I'm gone if I don't let her know what's happening to me. And I can't look Rudy in the eye. Hey-Soos has been telling me this all along. The thing that prevents the worst from happening is the truth. Rudy's just shown me that, loud and clear. You get that as advice from your parents when you're a little kid stealing candy, from your pastors, from your teachers, even if they don't practice it. It's the one thing you can't be wrong saying.

"I told myself a long time ago that if I ever felt that desire again I was gone," Rudy says.

"Well, you felt it and you're still here."

"I may not be for long."

A chill runs from my butt crack to my hairline. "Are you talking about, like, leaving or . . . "

"Ben, I *knew* what I was doing. I had firsthand experience being in his shoes. I knew the hate, I knew the self-contempt, and I knew the confusion. And I loved that kid; like a father loves a child; but I did it anyway, and he's gone. That's as close as you get to first-degree murder without pulling the trigger."

"Yeah, but . . . "

"You know what my church would have done? Demand I go on retreat and get counseling. Then they'd send me to a new parish." He shook his head sadly. "They're a church. They believe you can be cured through prayer." He throws up his arms. "So I ran."

I'm listening, but my mind is back there where he said *if I ever felt that desire again I was gone.*

"Look, Rudy," I say, "let's try something. I'm safe

because I know. That covers it for now. All you gotta do is stay here and do your job and teach me about Malcolm X and all the other good shit you know about the history you've lived through, so I can go to school and whack on the back of Lambeer's head. We'll take it a day at a time."

He walks slowly to the workbench and opens the sack, extracting a bottle of geezer vitamins and some flaxseed oil. He stares at the labels. "No guarantees," he says.

I drive toward home, thinking I got the best I could get. I suppose the thought of Rudy's possible death would scare me more if I didn't have my own to think about.

I drive up and down a deserted Main Street at maybe twenty miles an hour. The community Christmas tree stands decorated and alone in the middle of the street, a traffic hazard for sure. This time of year you could throw a sleeping bag under it at eight P.M. and not worry about anything until six or seven the following morning if it weren't for the freezing temperatures and the occasional possibility of a late-night snowplow. I turn up one side street after another, gazing at colored lights surrounding windows and the occasional dim bluish light of a TV playing. The living room light is on in Coach's house and I impulsively pull the pickup into his driveway. I sit a few minutes, contemplating going in. I know what I want to say, but I can't find a way to do it.

As I start the engine to drive away, his front door opens. "Hey! I'd recognize the sound of that engine anywhere. What happened, Ben, did my pickup finally find its way back home? Get in here."

I sit on the couch while he pours me a Coke and pops a beer for himself. He sits. "Talk."

I say, "Could I ask you some questions without you asking anything back?"

"Probably not," he says, "but I'll give it a go."

"Do you ever talk about your girlfriend?"

"Which one? I've had a lot of girlfriends. You mean Becky Sanders?"

I nod.

"I talk about her sometimes. There's not much to say." He sips his beer. "Biggest surprise of my life," he says. "Bigger than that catch you made in the Horseshoe Bend game. I swear, I'd already thought of a million ways I could lose her, mostly having to do with us going off in different directions after graduation, but I never thought a couple of shitheads playing on a dirt bike would get her."

"What was it like?"

"Like taking a shot to the ribs from a Reggie Jackson home run swing," he says. "My mom had to tell me. I was working at Dad's service station and I just left the place wide open and hauled ass for the bridge. The front of her car was nosed into the river. . . . " His voice trails off, then he shakes his head. "An old bartender named Dakota, guy missing one hand–had a hook–was there with the tow truck. I worked for him part-time at his bar when I wasn't working for Dad. He was kind of a mentor. Anyway, he stopped me from going down to the car, from seeing her." Coach takes another sip and smiles. "You know, we live in this high mountain air and it was one of those days when the sun was so bright you have to squint without sunglasses. But I swear, as I drove back into town, the entire world was dimmer. It was dim for a long time. It's still dim, I guess." He watches me playing with the ice in my glass. "What're you, writing a paper? What's up?"

I say, "Is there anything that would have made it better, *could* have made it better?"

"I don't know. I cursed God for not preparing me, but I don't know that you can prepare for that; maybe if someone you love has an illness, something you see coming. At least you'd be able to say good-bye; make sure everything was cool at the end. But no, I don't think there was a way to make it better. What's going on, Ben?"

I laugh. "I'll ask the questions here."

He laughs back. "Someone you know in trouble?"

"Not really," I say. "I don't know. There's this old guy. . . . "

"You talking about Rudy McCoy?"

"Yeah, kind of. He's been stopping drinking and stuff. Might not be in all that good a shape."

"Is he dying?"

"Naw. I mean, I don't know. He just got me thinking."

"I know this," Coach says. "Becky's dying wounded me. All I thought of was things I wished I'd said. I was a worthless date that first year in college, because I compared those girls to the *idea* of Becky; judged my relationships by how I felt with her, then I wouldn't hang in there long enough to let one get that far. I was probably kind of an asshole. It made me a fast runner, though."

"Do you think that's why you're not married now?"

He laughed. "I'd like to say no, but yeah. I know it is. I felt sorry for myself, got to thinking the only person who could understand me was me. Then I came back here and . . . Well, you've seen the middle-aged dating pool in this town."

"Think you'll ever beat it? Like go find someone?"

"Yeah, I do," he says. "I haven't told anyone, but I'm leaving after this year. I wanted to get you and your brother through school, and"–he laughs again–"see if I could help Boomer's kid turn out different from Boomer. Two out of three isn't bad."

"Thanks, Coach."

"You're not going to tell me what's going on, are you?"

"Naw. I mean, it's nothing. If it is, though, I'll tell you first."

"By the way," he says, walking me to the door. "Why don't you limit your Malcolm X issue to English class. Haley's *Autobiography* is a hell of a story and truly great literature, and you could avoid a war with Lambeer."

"If you're not in a war with Lambeer, his class is intolerable," I say. "He just tells you how things are. He has his point of view and the only way he validates you is if you see things his way. Funny thing is, the more you learn, the more you know how full of shit he is."

"I was afraid I'd get that answer. See you tomorrow." Coach isn't about to dis a teacher outright. He takes another sip of beer and lets the door slam behind him.

What I wanted from Coach was a glimpse of what it feels like to be left behind. I'm hardwired to sweat what's going to happen for Cody and Dallas (God, who'd have ever thought I'd get close enough to *her* to make a hole by leaving?) and my dad. There's no guessing what it will set off in Mom. And what about Coach? He sounds invincible to me most of the time, but he's had about as much sneak-up-behind-you death as he needs.

I drive back to the house and get on my winter running stuff and head out on a course I used for cross-country back in the day. I measured it by quarter miles so I could do interval training and measure my exact conditioning level, so I know exact distances. It runs a mile and a quarter along the highway toward Boise, veers off onto Cabarton Road for two and a half, makes a sweeping turn, and comes back home. It's cold outside so I use the first mile to get my legs warm, then shoot for full-speed half miles broken up with half-speed quarters. In my cross-country days, I'd go over the course two, even three times.

The warm-up mile tires me way more than it should, and I figure I'm simply not in top shape. The first full-speed half mile leaves my lungs burning so I take the first half-speed quarter mile more like quarter speed, and by the time I'm through the second half I'm thinking I get it that I'm not in great running shape, but football didn't end all that long ago and I've been running no less than four days a week. *It's starting.* I take the next quarter at a slow jog and try to kick in and there's nothing there and my heart starts to race and all of a sudden I hear myself screaming–I mean *screaming*–"No! No! Noooooooo!" and I'm lying in the snowbank sobbing, begging God for more time. I can't stop my racing heart and I'm thinking Doc didn't say anything about this shit giving me a heart attack before I realize it's panic; adrenaline. I lie there staring at the blanket of stars, wet cold seeping through my jacket, and take deep breaths between convulsions to slow my heart. I'm nearly soaked by the time I'm ready to get up, and I shiver and jog/walk to the house.

I run a hot bath, turn off the bathroom light, and sit in pitch darkness. I was going to tell. I really was: Dallas, Cody, Rudy, Coach, at least. But how can I do that now? I've talked myself into imagining dealing with them, but how can I deal with *me*? I feel my bravery leaking out into the warm bathwater. I can't let them see me weak. That would ruin everything.

Going out quietly is becoming a lot more complicated than I thought.

In the early evening on Christmas Eve my brother and I ride down to the football field to work on agility drills. I'm a few days away from my meltdown and I'm thinking—hoping—it was a false alarm. I woke up the next morning feeling pretty okay, and though I haven't tried anything quite that strenuous, I have taken a couple long slow runs and felt fine. I intentionally avoided calling up Hey-Soos that night, or since, because (and I know this is dumb) I didn't want even him to see me weak.

This workout may seem normal for a guy like Cody, getting ready to go on to a small-college football career, but remember it's December and Trout is a mile above sea level and Cody's working out two and a half hours a day at roundball. Above and beyond. So we dress up like we're headed to discover the South Pole except for our cleats, and hop into the Grey Ghost and head for the field. The good news is wind has blown most of the snow off the field. The bad news is the ground beneath it is rock hard.

Except for the lights from the Shell station across the street and the dim glow of a couple of distant street lamps, the field is dark so we leave the pickup running with the headlights pointed at a small section of the field; not the most conservation-minded thing to do with gasoline running close to the price of gold, but we promise to take cold showers and not turn on our electric blankets and leave our mother on an ice floe so we don't have to heat her room.

We take an easy six laps around the track to warm up, jogging through the glow of the headlights into the blackness at the far end and around again. I'm so relieved my strength feels normal. I run in front, Cody a couple steps behind with a ball. He yells, "Right!" and lobs it over my right shoulder, directly into my outstretched gloves. "Right!" and there it is again. "Left!" and I reach to the left, where the ball settles in. "Over the top!" and I stretch them out in front. The drill was created for receivers, but Cody uses it to hone his accuracy. He falls farther and farther behind me, still placing the ball perfectly 90 percent of the time. It's his show on the far end because I can't even see my hands. My brother has some feathery touch.

He talks as we jog. "It's gonna be great at Boise State with you, little big bro," he says. "You know it's not just the football. Right!" and the ball comes over my shoulder. "It's us, man. We can split the scholarship. We'll split the scholarship and the trust. Hell, with your brain you'll have an academic scholarship before the first year is out. What institution of higher learning is going to give you up? Left!"

Cody's right. It is *us*. We're the heart of the Wolfs, or better, the heart of the wolves. Dad's will drive that mail and freight route and take care of Mom until that turns out however it turns out. It's always been me and Cody and it will be me and Cody until the day . . . well, until the day.

I want to tell him but I can't. Not tonight. It's Christmas; Mom is out of the bedroom and has actually put up a few decorations. Dad is acting as if everything's perfect; got a tree, bought presents. Here on the track, the ball settles into my hands every time and I just don't want to feel the way I'm going to feel when I say it. Not yet. I wish I'd have said it right off, now. I wish I hadn't been so selfish as to think I could ask for a normal year.

Eighteen

"Man, why didn't you tell me what a stupid idea it was to try to keep this secret?"

"I believe I did hint at it."

"Yeah, but I mean, like, the first time you showed up. Why didn't you say it then? 'Ben, that's the dumbest fucking idea I've ever heard of.'"

"Have we talked about the appropriateness of certain language in the presence of a spiritual entity?"

"We have. And I'll hold back on the F bomb if you'll give me a quick heads-up when you see me diving into my own asshole. Here on earth we call that metaphor."

"Believe me, I know metaphor."

"So what about it? A deal? I clean up my potty mouth and you swim ahead and clear out the big logs?"

"I told you before, by request only. Don't you know anything about free will?"

"Wasn't he a killer whale some kid let go in a movie?"

"That's Willy," Hey-Soos says. "Get the free will thing down. It's the greatest thing about being human."

"So tell me."

"Well, basically if I knew everything that was going to happen, you wouldn't have free will, would you? What fun would that be?"

"If you knew it and I didn't know you knew it, I would."

"Nope. If anyone knows it, then it isn't free. It would mean that no matter what you do, things would have to turn out the way the person who knows how they turn out says they turn out."

"But God knows, right?"

"Nope again."

"God doesn't know how things turn out?"

"It knows that things turn out. Listen, Ben, I could spend a whole bunch of human time telling you how things are. But if your doctor's right, you'll know soon enough, okay? Let me satisfy your curiosity for now, and then let's stop talking about all this and live your life. God isn't a guy. God isn't a girl. God is a force. You have all these people trying to figure out whether to believe in God or the big bang.

Well, God is *the big bang. God is the ultimate scientist. If God relegated his thinking to human cognition, it would never get anything done. I mean, look how slow you think, and you're probably the smartest kid in your class. Just know that everything started as one, everything still is one, and it will end up as one."*

If there was any doubt that Hey-Soos is the inner part of me, which I've already said a thousand times there isn't, it is done. Once again he's gone *way* beyond my capacity to make shit up. WAY beyond. I gaze around the space we're in, which is basically my bedroom, only not. I've noticed this before, even when I was at Dallas's place. My furniture, my posters: all that shit is missing. There are only colors and it's like we're *in* them. I have to remember to ask about that sometime. Right now I have to get oriented.

"I feel like I should be asking about the meaning of life or something."

"You already did that," he says. *"Time wasted. You're playing a game. A beautiful, wonderful, hard, scary game. And you're gathering information from it."*

"For what?"

"To take with. Man, you are testing my patience."

Back on task. *"So you didn't tell me it was a messed-up idea to keep this all a secret because . . . "*

"Because experience is the only teacher," Hey-Soos says. *"Even if I could have told you, it would have been a lecture. Why do you think kids don't listen to their parents, or people don't leave churches and do what the preacher tells them?"*

Whew.

"There's only one thing that's universal."
"What's that?"
"The truth."

So now I have to figure out when and where to tell it. I could tell Lambeer, or Sooner. It'd make their day. I could tell my mother, who would probably become so depressed her heart would just stop beating; or Dad, and watch another two thousand pounds load onto his shoulders. I could tell Dallas, and stand there and watch my own heart break; or my brother, and feel the world cave in under both our feet.

In the end, I have to tell them all. But I know right where to start.

* * *

"Hey, man, you feeling any better?"

"That's relative," Rudy says.

"I think I know how to get us back on course."

"Great. Before you spring it on me, I need to say something."

"Shoot."

"You've been straight with me, now I have to be straight with you. I can't promise I'll stay."

I wait.

"Alive, I mean. I can't promise I'll stay alive."

Shit.

"There's no redemption for what I did. I can't give it back. I can't get Donny's life back; for him or for the people who loved him. I took his trust and I killed him. There's no way to fix that."

"Maybe–"

"No maybes. Some things can't be fixed." He looks at his hands, folded in his lap in front of him. "Do you have any idea what a horror it is to be me?"

Experience is the only teacher. "Nope," I say. "I don't. I couldn't. But look, Rudy, the reason I don't is that I didn't go through it. Somebody gets hold of you when you're a little kid and wrecks you, you grow up and wreck somebody, too. You didn't ask for that."

"But I knew."

"Yeah, you knew. And you've had nothing but shit ever since. But let me throw in what I came to say."

He shakes his head as if there's nothing.

"I can't promise I'll stay, either. In fact I can pretty much promise I won't."

"I don't expect you to keep comin' down here. Not after–"

"Alive," I say. "I can't promise I'll stay alive, either."

He looks at me dumbly.

"I got some shitty disease. This is it for me. This year. I think I can already feel it going."

He moves toward me, as if he wants to comfort me, then reels back.

"Don't worry. I've known all year. But look, it doesn't matter if you're, like, attracted to me because like I said, I could probably kick your ass and I know I can outrun you. You are safe for the first time in your whole life, Rudy McCoy, because I'm willing to live with whatever the fuck you did. I like you and I want you to help me mess with Mr. Lambeer so I can die happy. If you have fantasies about me, then you do. I'll pretend you don't. Just focus on me and not some other kid and I'll keep you in line, and we'll go one day at a time until there are no more days, and then if you want to off yourself, well, what the hell, I'll see you there." Man, I do not know where half of that came from, but the truth has the ring of truth to it so I know I'm right. All the regular bets are off when death has its arms outstretched.

"I'm not going to wait for an answer," I tell him, "'cause it would just mean you'd have to look like you were forgiving yourself, which I know you can't. So just fucking hang in here with me." I turn and leave.

Whew.

January 2

"Hey, Coach."

"Hey. My biggest little hitter."

"I'm here to come clean."

"Finally. Someone. Have a seat." He motions me to the chair next to his desk. First day back. School is over for the day; the classroom, empty.

"I'm dying."

"I know what you mean."

"No. I'm dying."

He searches my eyes. "Literally." He means it as a question.

"Literally."

He walks to the classroom door and closes it, returns slowly to his chair. "Talk to me."

"I've known all year," I say. "It's why I went out for football. I found out when I went for my cross-country physical last summer."

"What is it?"

"'Blood disease,'" I say, quoting Doc.

"Are you taking treatments? What the hell? What kind of doctor–"

"It's not his fault, Coach. He did everything he could to make me do this right–or the way you're supposed to. I'm eighteen. He had no choice."

"He sure as hell could have kept you out of football. All he had to do was not pass you on your physical."

I pinch the bridge of my nose, rub my eyes. "Coach, don't do this. I pled a hell of a case. And it was the right thing. Did I have a hell of a season or what?"

Coach sits back, places his mouth and nose on his finger tepee. I can see him running back over that senseless death more then twenty years ago. "That's just irresponsible," he says, more to himself than to me. He's stuck back on Doc.

"This is what I was afraid of."

His head snaps up.

"I could have set myself up for treatment, but . . . " I hesitate, but tell him anyway, that I knew this was my time, how I have never pictured myself past this place. "I knew I was done but I wanted it to be 'normal.' But then I realized there's nothing normal about cashing out at eighteen, and that a whole bunch of people I really care about deserve to know. I'm starting with you."

"Your parents . . . Cody?"

"No," I say. "Shitty as it probably is, you know about as much about death as anyone I know, so you're my first-round pick."

He sits, staring at his fingers. "Let me get this straight," he says finally, "you discovered sometime toward the end of summer that you have a terminal illness, had the presence of mind–if we want to call it that–to keep the doctor from telling anyone, turned out for football, and started hustling the sharpest girl in school?"

"That's about the small and short of it," I say.

"Jesus, Ben. That kind of changes the meaning of the phrase *death wish*. I don't know what to say. So we're halfway through the year and you decide to tell." He's quiet; exasperated.

Finally, "How can I help?" This is what I love about Coach. Tonight sometime the full reality will dawn on him, but he's like me: the guy you want at the site where the plane went down.

"The more I didn't tell people, the more complicated it got," I say. "I just wanted to have a normal last year; as close to normal as possible with, well, you know."

"But there was nothing normal about it," he says.

I nod. "One reason I came to you, besides that you've always been cool to me and my brother, is you haven't exactly had the best luck with death."

Coach smiles and looks down. "It kicked my ass right at your age," he says.

"I'm worried about the people I leave behind," I tell him.

"You came to the right place. I think you're right; you need to tell. Maybe not everyone, but the important people. When Becky died I could only think of all we never got to say. Ben, I'll help you with this any way I can. I just wish you'd told me earlier."

"If I'd told you, would you have let me play ball?"

He smiles. "Probably not."

"I rest my case," I say. "Catching that pass from my brother was the single most thrilling physical event I've had, and I've had sex. I wouldn't give it up for anything."

"I get it. So how can I help?"

"Just hang with me," I say. "I don't know how this is going to land. I've known for quite a while and when I tell Cody and my parents and Dallas"—I flinch—"it's going to be like everything I said since I found out is a lie."

"I'll be here," Coach says. "You know I will. And keep in mind, these are people who love you and they're smart. It might take them a while, but they'll understand. And if they don't, we'll make them understand."

Man, I hope he's right.

Nineteen

Coach was right that it wouldn't be brilliant to be indiscriminate in who I told, and that I should decide based on relationship. Cody and Dallas are shoo-ins. We disagreed on my parents. I don't want them broadsided when it hits, but at her worst my mother is crazier than Daffy Duck, and at her saddest she's the most guilty person in the world. It compromises my commitment to the truth, but it feels self-protective. Plus, I'm not telling the world in general because there's no point. Mom and Dad aside, you gotta care enough that I'm here now for me to tell you I'm leaving.

Meanwhile I want to get back to living. I gotta tell you, I think Lambeer may be a closet bigot and I don't think he keeps the closet door pulled all the way shut. It doesn't make sense he's fighting me so hard on this project unless he doesn't want Trout's response made public. Bottom line: racism is current. Bottomer line: all bigotry is current. Double bottom line to seal the two: Malcolm X traveled as far down that road as anyone.

Imagine if I could get the people of Trout, Idaho, to pay attention to the beauty of that larger world. Got legacy written all over it.

"Hey." Dallas is fixing pasta for Joe Henry as I come up behind her.

"Hey," she says back. "What's up?"

"Nothin' much," I say, and reach into the colander to snag a couple strings of spaghetti. "Want me to throw this against the wall for you?"

"Nobody actually does that," she says. "How come you're early? I thought you were going to let me get the booger-eater to bed."

Joe Henry's digging in his toy box for his baseball glove and Wiffle Ball. I've been preparing him for life as a jock. To my discredit, I've been doing it with all appearances of being around when he steps into that life. This is not going to be fun, but if I wait I'll chicken out.

"I've got some bad news."

She turns around. "Lay it on me."

"Well, it's like . . . I'm dying."

"Me too. What's the news?"

Jesus, is everyone going to say that? "No, I mean it. I'm dying. I've got this blood disease. . . . "

Her mouth actually drops open. "What? What kind of blood disease?"

"'Aggressive,'" I tell her, quoting Doc again. "I may only be good for most of this year."

She leans against the sink. Joe Henry hands me the Wiffle Ball and stands waiting with the glove.

"Just a minute, guy. I'll be with you in a sec."

"Oh my God, Ben, when did you find out? What are we going to do? Why aren't you in the hospital, or . . . "

Here comes the hard part. "I've known since summer. It's why I went out for football, actually. Doc Wagner caught it when I went for my cross-country physical."

She stares and I *know* all our conversations are running through her head; I can see the betrayal.

"I know this is going to sound stupid," I say, "but it made sense. I mean, the minute Doc said it, I knew it was right; like something I already knew and just needed it verified. One of those feelings."

"Oh God, Ben. What about treatment? I mean, why

aren't you . . . bald or something?"

"The specialist said it was as aggressive as any he's seen, that there was a *chance* it would go into remission, but realistically we could only buy a little time. I . . . I decided to play it out. I mean, I've been eating exactly right and–"

"You aren't trying to beat it?"

"Well, with nutrition, and, you know. But Dallas, I gotta tell you. Treatment means a whole different kind of life, and probably only a little longer one."

It hits her. "You knew you were dying when you started seeing me?"

I hang my head. "I couldn't imagine you'd like me," I say. "I mean, there was *no* chance. I thought I could play. Knowing I was dying made me brave."

"But then you slept with me. And I told you . . . and you *still* didn't say it?"

"It seemed too late." God, this is worse than I thought. I've done something really shitty.

In a low, calm voice, Dallas says, "Get out of here."

"Dallas, come on. . . . "

"Go. Do not come back. You turn around and put down that fucking ball and get out of here."

If you could hear her tone, you wouldn't argue, either.

● ● ●

I get in my pickup outside Dallas's house and just let it all wash over me. What in the world was I thinking? That was going to happen one way or the other, even if I decided to keep it quiet until I couldn't. There has to come a point when it *isn't* quiet.

God, how am I going to make it through the rest of this time without her? How am I going to do that? She'll be at school, at games. She'll be pissed, won't talk. I mean, if you want to see *resolve*, you want to see Dallas Suzuki on the volleyball court or the basketball court. This is not how I envisioned the last half of my year playing out. She wasn't just falling for me (how outrageous does *that* sound?); I was totally on my ass for her. This feels worse than dying.

It's dark outside and it's cold; I mean, headed for freezing and then way down below that. The big snows haven't started yet, but the last of them will melt close to Easter. But if it's not the Antarctic, I can run in it, and football hero or no, running's my thing. Nothing lets me focus better than the even beat of my feet pounding the dirt roads up around the lake. The house is quiet and I quickly pull on my sweats, cover them with Gore-Tex and slip out the back door. A dim light glows through Mom's window. She's lying there, staring at the ceiling, probably wishing she could trade places with someone like me.

On this moonless night, the Milky Way spreads across the sky like a billion fiery marbles. If it weren't for potholes, the roads around here would have no surface at all, so I run high on the left edge on hard-packed snow to avoid them, starting slow, worried my body might bail on me again. But in a mile or so I'm into a slow pace, and in two I'm wondering if other kids are like me. I don't mean other dying kids, and I know a lot are dying in lots worse ways than I am. I don't have to watch too much CNN to know that. But I wonder if other kids try as hard as I do to figure out who they are and why they're here. Adults talk about how kids' brains aren't fully developed and we're like bulletproof sociopaths or something, but that's not true, at least not for me. Most of us just have a hard time putting things into words. I consider this road I'm running on, bordering water for nearly fifty miles, frozen white just below the road's edge. Ride back twenty-some odd years and these are Coach's feet, pounding the dirt in the middle of the night, trying to soak up the meaning of life, when the most important one in his had been taken. It would have been spring; warmer, but he would have been staring up into the same Milky Way asking the same question I ask. How do I make it worth it?

When Doc gave me the news I thought it was all about me, but I was wrong. It's about me and everyone I touch. Looking back, I wish I had just said it and told anyone who felt sorry for me that I'd flatten their tires and run a pocketknife down the side of their car in the middle of the night if they patted my head even once.

I reverse my direction and head for home. I'm gonna need to be fresh in the morning to face Dallas–or to not face Dallas–and I've gotta tell Cody before it leaks out. If he finds out from somebody else, my life span will be halved.

"It's not getting simpler."

"You can say that again."

"If you weren't so messed up, I would," Hey-Soos says. "What did you expect?"

"Obviously I didn't know. As usual, I didn't think things out too far. Hey, I'm pissed at you. I thought if I told the truth, things would get clearer."

"They are *clear," he says. "They just aren't easy."*

"Man, I need you to walk me through this."

"That's why I'm here."

"I've been thinking about that. Why are you here? I mean why now, and why me?"

"Because you can use the help, and because you can take the help. And because giving to you, and to people like you, is my best way to spread truth."

I'll have to digest that. I say, "I went running tonight."

"I saw that. Wasn't it cold as hell? That's just an expression."

"Yeah, but you know me."

"That I do."

"I'm not having a lot of luck getting things to turn out the way I want them."

"You know what they say: if you want to give God a laugh, tell Him your plans."

"Well, I finally got it about telling the truth to everyone. So far it's not much fun, but I got it."

"It's easier if you tell it in the first place."

"Yeah, yeah, I got that part, too. You're not going to tell me how this turns out, are you? Like with Dallas, and my brother?"

"Nope. I told you, I don't know how it turns out."

"It would sure make it easier."

"And more boring. What would be the point of life if you knew how everything turns out? Just remember the more you act out of fear, the less you'll get done."

● ● ●

Mid-January

The Malcolm X Avenue idea doesn't sit a lot better with the voters of our fair county than it does with Lambeer. I think I know why he's considered such a good teacher in these parts.

"Good morning, Mr. Gardner. I wonder if you'd consider signing my petition to turn a street in our fair city into Malcolm X Avenue."

"Hey, Ben, how are you? What?"

"Malcolm X Avenue. I'm doing a project for my current events class. I thought Trout would look, like, seriously progressive if we took this diversity bull by the horns. Malcolm X Avenue would be a good start toward that."

Mr. Gardner looks over his glasses at me from behind the checkout counter at Gardner's SuperMart. "You talkin' about Malcolm X the Black Muslim nigger?"

I wince. "There's only one Malcolm X, I think."

"Got himself shot by a bunch of his own kind? That Malcolm X? Disrespected his people giving up his last name for an X?"

"That's the guy," I say.

"Ben, you made a lot of us proud on the football field this year, you really did. But if I were you, I'd let it go at that and keep this Malcolm X thing under your hat." He smiles. "Oh, I get it. This is a joke, right?"

"No sir, no joke. So I can put you down as a *maybe*?"

At the end of my first foray, I have one signature on my petition: Ben Wolf.

Twenty

I'm walking around school in a daze. Dallas is in most of my classes. She comes into homeroom late, leaves early, and somehow manages that for every class. She doesn't have to; I'm feeling crappy enough not to confront her and make this worse than it is. I'm also feeling physically crappy and I can't tell if that's because I'm dying because I'm dying, or if it's because I'm dying because I'm losing Dallas. I'm gearing up for Cody, which is giving my stomach fits, plus I need to go back and see how Rudy is.

I'm packing big attitude, because when I feel this crappy I'm combative as hell. I also wear my running stuff instead of regular clothes so I can take off any time I want; lunch, after school. Even if I can't run the way I used to, sanctuary these days comes with accelerated heartbeats.

"Hey, man, how come you aren't sitting with your honey?" Cody sets his lunch tray beside mine. I'm sitting alone, reskimming the section in *Lies My Teacher Told Me* that speaks to Woodrow Wilson's white supremacy. Cody takes the book out of my hand. "If it ain't subversive, you ain't readin' it, huh? Where's Dallas?"

"I think we're taking a break," I say. I meant to prepare him, but every time I started to bring it up, I was afraid to tell him why.

"A break? Who's dumb idea was that?"

I can't really lay it all on Dallas. "It was kind of mutual."

"No such thing," he says. "Which one of you said, 'I don't want to see your ass for a while'?"

I laugh. "She did."

"You want me to straighten her out?"

"God no." I say it too quick and too loud. "I mean, no. It was my fault."

"When did this happen?"

"The other night."

"The other night? Which other night? And you didn't tell me?"

Dolven and Glover plop their trays down, and

several other guys are headed this way. Dolven says, "The brothers Wolf."

"Hey, Randy," I say, then lower my voice at Cody. "I was trying to figure it out for myself. I was embarrassed. You know. . . . "

"Save your embarrassment for the shitheads," Cody says, smiling and nodding at Dolven and Glover. "You don't hide things from your bro. Together we're like a whole person." He watches me a minute. For some reason I can't find a way to act, and I'm staring at the table. "Hey, what's the matter, man? This feels serious."

"Buddy, we gotta talk."

Here's why my brother is going to be the best quarterback ever to pull on a helmet at Boise State. We're home when I finally tell him, sitting in his room after midnight under posters of Michael Jordan, Brett Favre, and Michael Johnson.

"You used to talk about dying young," he says.

I nod. "Um-hmm."

"You just decided on your own to let it ride." He says it as a statement, but it needs affirmation. I nod again.

"I might have done the same thing," he says. "I get it, at least. You know what I hate?"

I shake my head, afraid my voice will betray me.

"That you didn't think you could walk straight out of the doctor's office and tell me."

He's right. You know, you love your parents because they are who they are; maybe because they're a link to the generations before and most assuredly because if they're worth a shit they take care of you unconditionally. And you can love a girl almost to desperation. You can feel such a connection and such lust you think you can't live without her. But that heat cools, probably in order not to kill you. I have loved my brother without condition or consideration for more than seventeen years. There is not a day I can remember when I wouldn't have laid my life down for him, and that's not even an exaggeration. And there is not a day I can remember that I believe the same isn't true for him. I'm not a camo-fatigue kind of guy, but I would go into any war with either of two people: my brother or Coach Banks.

Cody says, "I've got your back. Hell, I'll even help you get the Malcolm X thing done. Too bad it's not still football season; we could threaten to throw a game unless they voted for it." He's sitting on the edge of his bed; I'm standing in the doorway. He pats the bedspread beside him, and I sit. He puts that big ol' football throwin' arm around my shoulder and I just lean into him. I can feel his cheek on top of my head. "Man, I can't wrap my mind around this, and who knows, I might beat you half to death when I do, but we'll get through it. What are you gonna do about Mom and Dad?"

"I gotta sit on it a while," I say.

"I'll follow your lead," he says. "It'll be like football."

Cody and I sit longer while I swim in regret for not telling him right away. He's right: together we make a pretty good man. It's always been like that.

We talk for a while about the nuts and bolts of it; that I've felt pretty good all along; though I *think* I've had some drops, it might just be paranoia. I don't describe the one bad night run. I swear I think if I don't talk about it, I can make it disappear. I've been eating right and taking all these nutrients; keeping my body high on pH and low on acid, working out. If I'm around this time next year, I'll be at BSU with him.

"Man, I'm going to miss you in football," he says. "I can't believe this."

"Just listen for me in your head."

He hits his chest with his fist to let me know where he'll listen for me.

● ● ●

I am getting zero sleep, which can't be good for the terminally ailing. But I'll feel like I can't keep my eyes open five more minutes, like a while ago with Cody, and three hours later I pop awake. I know it won't last all that long, but I also know I won't be able to sleep until that tiredness hits me again, so I might as well make use of the time.

"Hey, Rudy." It's three A.M.; pitch-dark. I can come here at any time of day or night and find him puttering somewhere in the garage or reading in his little room, or doing whatever keeps him from going back to the bottle, but there's not even light through the crack. I feel along the walls for the switch and turn the overheads on long enough to draw a bead on the small lamp sitting on the workbench. I flip them off quickly and feel my way to it, screw in the small bulb, casting the inside of Halls Garage in a dim, eerie glow.

"Hey, Rudy," I say again.

I should let him sleep—he gets so little—but I'm feeling urgent lately, so I knock lightly on his door. "Rudy. Hey."

The door opens into blackness and I reach around the corner and flip that switch. The 40-watt bulb flickers on and there's Rudy, lying on the bed fully dressed, eyes closed, hands folded over his chest. He's not breathing. There's a small stack of books by the cot, *The Autobiography of Malcolm X* on top, with an envelope sticking out just inside the front cover.

I don't wonder even for a second, just step over and take the envelope. It says BEN like I knew it would. I touch his hand, which is cold. He's been like this awhile.

Rudy's my first dead guy. My first thought is I'm gonna look just like this soon. It's not so bad; he took pains not to look ghoulish, I think. Eyes closed. He looks calm and I realize it's the first time I've seen that. His face is dead, but it's not tortured. Man, I am walking through shit I have never walked through before.

I could leave; slip out with the envelope and the books, and let the Hall brothers find him later this morning, but that doesn't seem right. I set this in motion, so no point in giving them the big surprise.

I switch off the light in Rudy's room, leave the workbench light on, and take the books to my pickup, where I call 911 on my cell. That gets me Ed Sorensen over at the firehouse.

"Nine-one-one."

"Hey, Ed. It's Ben Wolf."

"Hey, Ben. Trouble?" His voice is scratchy, like the call woke him.

"Yeah, kinda. I think Rudy McCoy committed suicide. He's over at Halls. I stopped in to see him and he's lyin' there on his bed. I think he's been dead awhile."

"What makes you think it's suicide? He probably drank himself to death."

I'm about to start into a long explanation, but I don't have the energy. "Maybe," I say. "It's just a guess. There was no bottle. Anyway, he's there."

"I'll get someone right over there."

"Do I need to stay? I mean, I found him but I'm not going anywhere and I need to grab an hour or so of sleep before school. It would be a lot easier if I could talk about it later."

"Get some sleep, Ben. What the hell are you doing up at this time, anyway?" He doesn't wait for an answer. "Stop by the courthouse later and talk with the sheriff. I don't guess there's much to this. Ol' Rudy never did have much but his books and his drink."

He had a lot more than that.

It's a couple hours before the sun comes up and I'm just not sleepy, but as crazy as things have been and as crazy as they're going to get, it would probably be good if the members of my family woke up and found me where I'm supposed to be.

I fall into bed in a heap, but no way do I try to rest before reading his words.

Dear Ben,

I'm sorry, but I couldn't do it. I know you could have kept me safe around you; hell, I could have kept myself safe. But I couldn't go on living with this thing inside me, because it's deadly poison. It took everything from me. If I had done a better job when I was in the church, I might understand better. But I was afraid all the time; in my heart praying for myself instead of others. I looked to God to save me, but He just looked back and shrugged. I'd have done what was right if I hadn't been so afraid. In the end, it just feels better to be gone. Know that as I write this letter, I feel tremendous release. I don't know what happens next, but I'll damn sure guarantee you it's better than this. I wish I had more courage, but I never had much and it's all used up.

Go out there and kick some ass, young fella. You're truly one of a kind. I enjoyed my time with you and that's saying something, since I haven't enjoyed much of anything for the past many years. Learn all you can about Malcolm X and all the other tremendously brave people of all colors and run them down your teacher's throat. Run 'em down the throat of the town. Those who finally get it will thank you, and those who don't, well, they weren't gonna get it anyway.

Please understand that I know suicide is stupid and cowardly, and I'm apologizing to you. You've certainly facing your situation better than me. If it weren't for you, no one would be affected by my death and no one would care. That's not me being pitiful; I've purposely kept folks away. I didn't leave anyone else anything to miss. I'd appreciate it if you didn't tell anyone what I did; I hate leaving that bad taste in the mouth of the world. If you feel you need to, then go ahead.

And thanks for seeing me.

Rudy McCoy

I read it over twice. Man, it is hard to tell what's good from what's bad when you're in the middle of it. You don't have to watch too many episodes of *Law and*

Order: Special Victims Unit to know sex offenders are about the lowest thing this society has to offer. In prison they're rumored to be below armed robbers and murderers, but Rudy didn't seem like that kind of low guy. He just seemed sad. I should probably feel worse than I do, but it wasn't an impulsive act. Rudy was done. He looked at his situation the best way he could and opted out. I can't judge that. Truth is, I feel some release reading the letter. I'll do as he asks: keep his secret to myself. I'll keep the letter to read a few more times to see if I missed anything, then make sure I throw it away so nothing comes out after I'm gone.

Twenty-One

On my way to school I stop by the county courthouse to tell Sheriff Osborne what I know about Rudy McCoy.

"Ben Wolf. Great catch in the Horseshoe Bend game. Too bad you guys couldn't have taken them Indian boys out up at Weippe."

I say, "Little too much for us that day, Sheriff."

"So you were the last person to see Mr. McCoy alive."

"Actually, I'm not sure. I was the first person to see him dead, though. He was gone when I got there."

"What were you doing there that time a' night?"

I shrug. "Actually it was that time of morning. I was helping Rudy stop drinking. I've been taking him food and supplements for a while."

"Supplements?"

"You know, vitamins and other stuff I thought might make him feel better."

Sheriff Osborne smiles. "Quite the little social worker, huh?"

"I guess. Is there anything I need to do? When I called Nine-one-one Ed told me to stop in and see you."

"You just walked in and found him layin' there?"

"Yup."

"Hell, I'll just write it up and be done with it. Thanks for stoppin' in, Ben. That really was a hell of a catch."

"Thanks."

My catch in the Horseshoe Bend game is a bigger deal than Rudy McCoy's life.

I drive the three blocks to school and sit in the Grey Ghost, steeling myself to endure, yet one more time Dallas Suzuki gliding past me as if I don't exist. I'd do anything for a do-over, but, at least in this dimension, time marches on. I blew it and it remains blown.

I sit awhile longer today because I've started having these little "episodes" where fatigue just washes over me. They pass fairly quickly, though, so I lean my head against the back window and close my eyes and let my body catch up.

●　●　●

In Lambeer's class I can't stop thinking about Rudy, unable to wrap my imagination around his being gone because pretty soon I'll be gone, too. I can't help but think a compassionate universe is giving Rudy a breather. It seems his fate was set back in his childhood when he was molested, and the rest of the shit that went on in his life was going to happen unless somebody stepped in, and no one did. The one place he thought he could go to be safe was a trap. I think about all these Catholic priests who are in trouble today and wonder how many of them scrambled for the same sanctuary. Things can't be neat and tidy in the way most religions present them. You just can't get relativity out of black and white.

Dallas sits a few seats away, scribbling in her notebook as Lambeer talks, and I want to run over and beg her for another chance. I hear not one word of his lecture.

I can't concentrate in class, but I can keep the project going, so after school I grab my petition sheet and go see if I can get a name on it that doesn't end in Wolf.

"Benny boy, you remind me of my old hippie days," Rance Lloyd says. "Did some serious peyote. I thought Malcolm X was about the gutsiest black man ever to walk the face of this earth. By the time he got rollin' you could have just flipped a coin to guess whether another black man was gonna get him, or a white man. He was smart, and my God, could he talk. But here's the deal, son. I don't see any names on your petition there, and I'm guessin' I'm not your first stop. So tell you what. If you get to the place where you just need one more signature to put you over the top, you bring it back and I'll be happy to sign it. But my name alone on that page could cost me some business." Rance runs an antique shop and he subs for my dad driving mail and freight when Dad has more on his plate than he can chew. Rance also builds cabinets and remodels houses. It makes sense that politics plays into his decision.

"I got a feeling this first signature is going to be hard to come by," I tell him. "Thanks, though."

"You're doin' this for school? I got a feelin' your project is gonna be a dissertation on why you *couldn't* get a groundswell goin' for Malcolm. You have a particular street in mind?"

I point to the heading on the petition.

"Jackson Street? Jesus, Boomer Cowans lives on Jackson Street." Rance gets a serious belly laugh out of that. "Mind if I tag along when you knock on ol' Boomer's door? I ain't seen a human being killed since Vietnam."

That's funny. "I thought I'd just go ahead and slip his name into the "no" column."

"Well, if you get the signatures, you better slide yourself into the 'gone' column."

I certainly know the outcome to this academic adventure. Petitioning to make Jackson Street into Malcolm X Avenue is *Saturday Night Live*–caliber folly. But as I've said, you can do what you can do, and as bad as I'm feeling about Dallas it makes sense to court danger. It helps keep my mind off her, if only for fleeting moments. I was so selfish.

Malcolm X is teaching me so much about baby steps in the universe. Let's say I follow through and get no signatures and no street gets named after him—duh!–but I write a hell of a paper. I mean a *hell* of a paper. Lambeer won't read it, but I could give a copy to Coach and tell him to put it in the archives or the senior time capsule. Let's say he does, and let's say some kid picks it up when they start looking at that stuff a generation from now and nobody around this hick town knows Malcolm X from *Malcolm in the Middle.* But let's say this kid gets interested. And instead of a Ben Wolf he's a Cody Wolf and he says, "Listen to me or I won't throw any more balls for you," or better, "Name a street after Malcolm X or I'll tank the state championship." And he gets something started that stresses a little less hate. I wouldn't have done anything for the world, but I'd have done something for Trout, Idaho. And maybe somebody else will take it out of Trout to the world and run into the other folks who won't let Malcolm die. Just because I don't have lots of time doesn't mean there isn't lots of time.

Today I'm going to get my head back into things. I walk into Lambeer's class and put my head on my desk, focusing. Lambeer finishes taking roll and says, "So, Mr. Wolf, how many signatures have you gotten on your petition so far?" and I realize Trout is so small he's heard I'm truly going ahead with this project that is certain to earn me an F.

"What you should be asking is how many times I've heard the word *nigger* since I've been on the campaign trail."

"You will not use that language in my class, Mr. Wolf. You know better than that."

"Don't confuse the message with the messenger," I say back. "And get ready because you'll see it in my paper."

"I won't see anything in your paper because I'm not going to read your paper. It's obvious I can't stop you but I certainly don't have to be complicit. And I better not hear that word in my classroom again. You'll call it 'the *n* word.'"

"So it won't sound as nasty as it is?"

"You might want to think twice about pushing me, Mr. Wolf. I've recalculated the respective weights of the separate course requirements, and it's possible you could squeak by with a D. But you will be civil to me and others in this classroom or I will expel you from it. My wish to see you graduate aside, I have my limits."

"What if I don't care if I graduate?"

"If you don't care whether or not you graduate, just keep it up. You also might think about applying for Rudy McCoy's old job, because that's what you'll be qualified to do."

I mumble, "What a dick," under my breath.

"Excuse me?"

"If any of us did our jobs half as well as Rudy did his, we might learn the real details worth knowing in here.

Sylvia Longley, who I am coming to know and hate, says, "Mr. Lambeer, get rid of him. He's ruining this class."

To which Dallas replies, "Shut up, Sylvia, before I

treat myself to something I should have treated myself to a long time ago."

Whoa!

Dolven says, "Go Dallas!"

Dallas shoots Dolven a look and he sticks his nose back in his book.

"I think this might be a good time for you to take leave, Mr. Wolf. We'll talk about your future at a later date."

Cody slams his book shut and says, "Okay, but I don't see what I did."

That gets a laugh. Even Sooner thinks that's funny.

"Not you! Ben, go to the library."

I'm already loading my books into my backpack. I do need to get out of here. I almost ran over and hugged Dallas when she threatened Sylvia, a move that could have shortened my life expectancy.

Away from the chaos, I take inventory. I know I shouldn't lay it on Lambeer, but I think one reason I'm being such a shithead is I have put off telling my mother and father the bad news; told myself they'd be better off not knowing. But there's no way around it. If I'd been up front with Dallas things would be okay with her and me, I'll bet, and when I think about it rationally I was never in trouble with my brother and Coach, though it *was* smart not to tell either of them before I got my hands on a football, so, all things considered, I could make a case for having waited. But all my trouble so far has come from being the little control freak I am, deciding who should hear what when and trying to control other people's emotions by what I say. It's become clearer and clearer it's just disrespectful to not let people deal with things in a straightforward manner. When I'm lying on that bed on my last day, I want a clean slate.

I'm sitting in my mother's bedroom with Dad. Mom lies with her back to us, but I checked; her eyes are open. Dad's in the chair at the end of the bed. He doesn't know yet, but he knows this is important because no way do I bring him in here with me under normal circumstances.

"Mom, I know you can hear me, but you don't have to answer. I just can't keep what I have to say inside any longer. I want to apologize to both of you for not saying it sooner, but I had this dumb idea it was better not to."

Mom doesn't move, and Dad's brow is furrowed. Cody's not home; I wanted to make sure nobody accused him of inaction in the face of crisis.

"When I went for my cross-country physical this year,

I found out I'm sick. Terminal. It's aggressive and there's not much chance I'll live much past this year. . . . "

An involuntary moan escapes Dad's lips. He starts to rise but his knees buckle and he sits back down. I don't detect movement from my mother. "It's not your fault that I didn't say anything. I thought I could make my life normal. I threatened Doc Wagner that if he broke confidentiality I'd go after him legally. He did go ahead and pass me on my physical so I could play football, but I begged him and he was just trying to give me a break."

"Oh my God, Ben. What . . . I mean, what are they doing about it?"

This is the hard part. "I decided against that," I say. "It was going to make me sick, and I know this sounds really strange, but I just didn't think it would do any good and I wanted to have as healthy a year as I could."

My mother's shoulders start to shake and I lean over far enough to see her expression is blank but tears soak the sheets. Dad moves to the bed, wraps his arms around her shoulders and holds her while she silently sobs. His voice quivers as he whispers, "Go on, son. I'll handle this."

And I walk out of the room.

Twenty-Two

At least they know. I've said before it's crazy that I feel guilty about my loved ones feeling bad when I'm the one who's dying, but I'm hardwired that way. Things are clearer now, though; not easier, but clearer. The truth really does bring freedom. For one thing you don't have to remember which lie you told.

This disease is showing itself more regularly. What I felt that night on the run and to a lesser degree in the pickup can't be ignored. I've got no time for denial. I've had a couple of days just sitting through classes trying to build the energy to get to the next one. When that happens I double up on the supplements and catch every nap I can—thank God for math and Spanish. Coach gave me a key to his office in the gym so I can rest there, and he

covers for me in the teachers' lounge. I've stayed home a
few times, laid in bed and let the day go by while I gathered strength. Doc helps me out with some super boosters
so potent I don't even ask about them, and for the major-
ity of the time I'm okay; I just have these dips. Sometimes
when I'm home or just kicking back in Coach's office, I
get on the phone to see if I can drum up some signatures
for my Malcolm X petition, but mostly what I get are stats
for my paper on the number of times I hear "that word."

When Dallas walks into a room I tell myself we're like
ants on an anthill and the loss I feel doesn't amount to
anything in the cosmos. But the emptiness and the longing are so great I can't hold that thought and I begin to
wonder what's big and what's little. I have that program
in my computer where you look at the Milky Way from
such a distance it seems like one small star, then you start
clicking and getting closer and closer and pretty soon
you're looking at the solar system and then Earth and
then some clump of trees and when you're finished you're
staring into a single cell and it takes only a little imagination to realize that if the program kept going you'd be
inside an atom. The distances across that atom, in *relative*
measure, are the same as the distances across the universe.
So there is no big and no little and I'm left to realize that

the pain I feel, relative to me, is as big as two galaxies moving apart in the universe, and I can only come to the conclusion that the desperation I feel is huge.

I think about Dallas's uncle and I hate him; hate the visuals of him creeping into her room, or scaring her into not telling. I think of the betrayal, how tough it would be to trust anything if that happened to you. If you can't trust the people in your own family to keep you safe, your sense of trust would have to head right down the shitter. But then I think of Dallas with Joe Henry, the result of all that betrayal; how she just loves him and wouldn't give him up for anything and things get complicated. Rudy betrayed a kid, like, *cubed*, and that kid is gone and there have to be people everywhere that, if they knew it, would have come after Rudy with torches in the night. But what about Rudy McCoy when he was a little kid, suffering that same betrayal, then betrayal of a God that was supposed to keep him safe? I can't help but like him and I can't help but hurt for him and I can't also help but think if he were alive I'd do whatever I could do to keep him away from kids, and if I couldn't do that I'd have to turn him in because that is the *only* way you get this shit stopped.

Planet Earth is a tough town.

"This isn't turning out the way I wanted it to." My time in this half-awake cocoon of my room has become my greatest sanctuary.

"Really?"

"I actually thought Rudy was a guy I could save, thought he could get his redemption from me."

He smiles. "He was hardwired, as you put it, to be the way he was. Every time he came out of his stupor, his history was waiting for him. He mistook what he did for who he was. But he faced it and made his decision. You were way too late for Rudy, Ben. But you gave him some days he'd never have had without you."

"Yeah, but don't I get a break here? I mean, look at my mother. Talk about hardwired."

"I'd have to agree with you there."

"Man, who comes out of this?"

"Whoever chooses to. Listen, Ben, wise men and women have come here for centuries and left what they knew. In their time. Jesus, Buddha, Muhammad, Gandhi, Aloysius, Martina, Suddahara . . . "

"Aloysius? Martina?"

"Not all of them were famous. At any rate, all of them knew connection is everything and life is risky. They knew the *rule of joy and fear. They knew nothing dies. They knew the big bang; that some version of everything is inside you. Life is your practice field. The state playoffs are inside you.*

"Your first therapist, Marla, was right when she said her best advice comes from a flight attendant. Put your own oxygen mask on before you try to help anyone else. There's only one person you and I can save together, Ben, and when I leave that person will be the only one left in the room."

And Hey-Soos turns and walks away. I have a feeling I won't see him again until the moment I . . . change.

"Hey."

"Hey, Ben." Dallas stands behind her screen door beside Joe Henry, who wants the hell out to come play with me.

"Ben! Ben! Hey, Ben! Should I gets my glove?"

I watch Dallas. She watches me.

"Can I, Dallas Suzuki? Can I gets my glove and go play catch?"

"You'd better let him," I say. "It will make your evening easier."

"Go get your glove," she says. "And put on warm clothes."

Joe Henry disappears, while Dallas and I watch each other through the screen door.

"I didn't know what else to do," I say. "It was wrong not telling, but it seemed right at the time. I was selfish. And I know it was seriously messed up not to tell you after you told me everything, but I just got scared, like way more scared than of dying because I wanted it so much. But I don't think we should spend this time being mad at each other." It all comes out almost without punctuation, as fast as I can say it.

Dallas doesn't move. "I don't know, Ben. I don't know if I can. . . . "

I can feel my shoulders sink. "Okay," I say. "At least let me play catch with Joe Henry."

"You can play catch with Joe Henry," she says, then turns and disappears into the darkness of her living room.

It is freezing cold and Joe Henry bursts onto the porch so bundled up I don't worry about hurting him with the ball. He drops every throw, partially because he has mittens under his baseball mitt and partially because when he catches his next ball it will be his first, but he is undeterred. He runs after it and picks it up and throws it back over my head.

I don't even see Dallas in the window; I've done what I can and hope Joe Henry remembers me and says my name when he's my age and brings her back in time. Hey-Soos is right. You put yourself out there in the truest way you can and hope others do the same. You'll connect or you won't, but you did what you could. It's like playing ball in some way. There are guys on the team, like Cody, I'd give my life for. But you have to be willing to lay down your body for *all* of them if you want to put the best *you* on the field. Every guy on that team has to believe you'll bring nothing back off the field with you. If you do that, a few others will do the same and those who don't will go further than they would have. A team is a single thing, just like each of us is our arms and legs and brains and spirits. When one component isn't working, we're not at full speed. Same thing with the team of me and Dallas and Joe Henry. Right now one component isn't working, and if we went into a competition we'd lose. But I've left it all on the field.

Mid February
"You've missed two classes this week, Mr. Wolf," Lambeer says.

"Excused absences," I say back.

"I thought you might have gone out of town to get your signatures."

"No way, man. My project is scientific; works no matter how the electorate responds."

"I hope you're not going to try to put a bigotry label on your hometown."

"Good research is like good journalism," I say. "Just the facts. I'll let the reader put the label on. And since you're not reading it, there won't be any readers. Trout is safe."

"I just hope you remember we owe something to the place we're from."

"What do I owe?"

"Some allegiance, maybe some appreciation. You wouldn't be who you are if it weren't for the people you grew up with."

"The good and the bad, right?"

Lambeer stares, waits.

"I mean if the good stuff rolls downhill, so does the shit, right?"

"Watch it."

"The bad stuff, then," I say, but I don't drop my gaze.

"I'm telling you, you want to think twice before you turn your back on your own home."

"And I'm telling you that if you think I'm turning my back on my own home by doing a survey, then you don't think much of my home, which if I remember right is your home, too. Look, Mr. Lambeer, we get educated so we can gather information, right? And so we can discriminate between the kinds of information we get. What other reason is there to get educated? Gather information and go out into the world with it. We learn math so we don't have to guess; we can be exact. Same thing with science. We learn history and literature to know the truth about those times. That is, *if* the people who are teaching us want us to know the truth."

"Young man, are you saying I'm not here to give you a proper education?"

I wonder if any adult ever called any boy "young man" without ill will. I'm not counting "He's a nice young man" because that's a description. I'm talking about, "What was that for, young man?" (my dad); "You get over here right this minute, young man!" (my mother); "What's gotten into you, young man?" (teachers, parents—mine and others—Sunday school teachers, pretty much anyone over the age of about thirty-five).

"I'm not saying anything about you, Mr. Lambeer. I'm really not. But I'm talking about education in general. Did you know almost every truly forward thinker in history was ridiculed, if not threatened, if not killed? You know why? For messing with current, *uninformed* beliefs. Galileo, Newton, Jesus, Darwin, even Einstein. Look at what's going on in the Middle East. All the fighters there, including us, have some big-time belief system we're touting and we're all willing to kill the hell out of the other side to make our point. And I get it. Their bad guys are way worse than our bad guys because they aren't afraid to die, but they aren't afraid to die because of some dumb belief that if they get martyred they're gonna get a bunch of stuff in heaven that most people don't get, like a whole bunch of virgins and shit. . . . "

"Ben . . . "

"And look at you. You think if you let me say that word the world is going to cave in or something. I'm on a totally uninformed tirade here and you're waiting to pounce on one bad word because it offends *your* belief system."

"Ben Wolf, you're not exactly Galileo or Newton and you sure as the devil aren't Jesus. Are you drawing parallels between your introduction of Malcolm X to Trout,

Idaho, with Newton and gravity? Are you that much smarter than the rest of us? Give me a break. There's a lot more behind those belief systems than you're allowing. There are good and evil in the world, and part of education is learning what they are."

Sooner says, "We got us a midget Einstein. Whoa."

I may not *be* Einstein but I'm smart enough to let that statement pass. "There may be good and evil," I say to Lambeer, "but neither you or I know what they are."

The vein in Lambeer's neck pushes against his shirt collar like a rat being devoured by a snake. "Maybe you don't know what they are, Ben Wolf, but I sure do."

"I think not," I say. This dying thing makes me way brave. "Let's say you're a five-year-old kid outside Da Nang, Vietnam, sometime in the late sixties or early seventies and fire comes raining out of the sky on your house. And I mean *fire. Raining.* You didn't do anything to bring that kind of shit–*stuff*–down on your head but happen to be inside your Vietnamese mother five years ago, and before the day's over you don't have that mother anymore and your face is burned beyond recognition. Somehow you live and forty-odd years later you're sitting around, burned and broken, wishing you hadn't had to grow up an orphan. Let's say you defied the odds and learned to read English and you pick up Robert McNamara's book like I did last month, and discover the United States had no idea what we got ourselves into when we went to war there because we didn't learn about the people. Robert McNamara was the secretary of defense then. They called him the *architect* of that war. Robert McNamara was the architect of a war he didn't understand and because he didn't *educate* himself, you got fire rained on you. Who are you going to believe is evil? And who can argue with you?"

"I can argue with you. My father fought in that war. You know nothing about Vietnam. Men put their lives on the line and came back home to ridicule and hate."

I'm tempted to reintroduce Lambeer to the term *nonsequitur*; tell him he's proving my point, but I'm zoned in. "No offense, but if I know nothing there's a pretty good chance you don't, either. I read about that war and I've heard about it from you. You read about it and heard about it from your dad. Neither of us knows what it was like to be there. My only point is that a lot of things happen because of faulty information and the reason to get educated is to cut down as much as possible on faulty information, not skirt it because we don't want to offend the locals."

The class is *silent*. They sense danger. But when you're dying, there is no danger. The truth works on every level, and I'm in a spot where I feel addicted to it.

Lambeer backs up a little, setting back my dooms-day clock a couple of seconds. "I won't get into my personal losses with that war," he says. "But history tells us that democracy gives people their best chance at having a good life. When you live in the best one in the world, arguably the best one in history, you have to back it through its mistakes as well as its triumphs."

"My country, right or wrong?" I ask.

"My country, right or wrong," he says.

"But if you're a patriot in whatever country you're in, that's true, right? I mean if you were a North Vietnamese you'd be considered a coward if you turned and fought for the U.S. Right? And if I live in Trout, Idaho, I can never see eye-to-eye with anyone from Harlem." In my defense I do see the differences; but I also see the similarities.

Lambeer has clearly had about enough of me. "You think you're pretty smart, Mr. Wolf, but there are things you don't understand. Things that come with experience. It's easy to pass judgment on your country and on free-dom when you're ensconced in a place it can't be taken away. But you're missing something important, something I probably won't convince you of today. You're missing experience. You're showing off in front of your friends because there's no cost. And I'm supposed to sit here and listen to your drivel because you're a student and I should be happy that you are curious, but I find your ideas sophomoric and ill thought-out, sir, and until you have that experience, I suggest you choose your words carefully so I'm not forced to put you in your place."

This is the time. "You're right, Mr. Lambeer. I do think I'm pretty smart. No Galileo, but pretty smart. And I'm going to have to go with that because I won't be getting the experience you're talking about."

"And why is that?"

"Because I'm dying. Because this time next year I'll be a picture in last year's yearbook. I want any information I get between now and then to be correct, which is why I'm all over the place with my arguments and why I'm busting your chops. And I'm pretty sure if you spend your lunches in the teachers' lounge you're hearing I'm the same pain in the butt in every other class."

I can *feel* the shock among my classmates. My brother is shaking his head and smiling. Dallas Suzuki stares at her desk. If I could know only one thing, it would be what she's thinking.

"What do you mean, you're dying?" Lambeer says. I put him in this tough spot on purpose.

"I mean no breathing, stopped heart, all stiff and stuff."

"That's not funny."

My brother almost spits out his gum. "It's not funny to me most of the time, either," I say, nodding at Cody. "Right now it kind of is."

"I'm going to end this discussion," Lambeer says. "It seems to have drifted."

I agree it's drifted.

Twenty-Three

Sweet Hey-Soos, who should I tell? Should I tell one? Should I tell three? What the hell, tell 'em all. All that contemplation, then I open my mouth and out come the beans. Two periods after I said it the whole school knew the hand I've drawn, and students walked around me like I had anthrax powder on my shoes, proving I wasn't *that* far from correct with my original decision. Cody hung with me. Dallas disappeared. I think she went home.

But file *this* under If You Want to Give God a Good Laugh . . . I walk into school a couple of minutes before class this morning to find the halls quiet as a church. I'm egotistical enough to think it's about me until I catch a glimpse of Mr. Cowans sitting in the principal's office, his forehead pressed against the flat surface of Mr. Phelps's desk, his body convulsing.

Sooner Cowans was killed last night. Car wreck. Not far from the bridge where Becky Sanders died during Coach's senior year. Just a random, senseless accident. Sooner took Ellen Marker, the girl who stood him up for homecoming, for a late burger at Clear Creek Station, which is about seven miles out of town. Mrs. Olsen fell asleep driving from town to the Olsen ranch about a mile past Clear Creek. She drifted across the yellow line and hit Sooner and Ellen head-on. Dead on impact. Mrs. Olsen has a sprained back and a couple of bruises.

Mr. Phelps stands with a microphone in the center jump circle before a stunned, silent student body. I can't help thinking the only person rude enough to make a noise in this tomb is the reason we're here. This exact same scenario is playing out over in Council, for a girl who was tough enough to hang out with Sooner.

Mr. Phelps starts to talk, chokes, and takes a deep breath. He tries again, gets a couple of syllables out, stops, covers his face. Coach steps up, gently elbows Mr. Phelps to the side.

"Listen, you guys. This is a big hit. One of you who

was alive yesterday is gone today. Simple as that. There's no way to sugarcoat it or make it better. A great kid is gone. In Council they're feeling exactly the same.

"We'll go ahead to class. Individual teachers will decide what to do with the time. Don't be surprised if most of the day is study time. Or sitting time. Or thinking time. The Boise School District is sending a couple of counselors for those of you who feel the need, and teachers will be available to talk during their free periods."

Coach lowers his eyes. "Guys, this is tough. The spirit and memory of Sooner will walk with us for a long time." He shakes his head. "This is senseless." He waves us to class.

As Cody and I rise to leave, I glance through the bleachers for Dallas, but she's not there. "I gotta get out of here, man. No way am I sitting through this day."

Cody says, "Want me to go with?"

"Naw. I'm okay. I'll probably run. Or walk. Whatever I can do. I *know* you don't want that."

He smiles and slaps my back gently. "Holler if you need me. My cell is on. Can't imagine anyone will give a shit. Can't imagine I'd care if they did."

● ● ●

Dad's in the backcountry with the mail and freight and Mom's door is closed. I slip upstairs and shove my iPod into the computer to make a playlist for loss. I start and end it with the song I found the day I heard from Doc what lay in store for me, the one I listened to on the hill; *Too Old to Die Young.* I've since discovered Ann Savoy wrote it. She sings it with Linda Ronstadt. The lyrics beg for time. Sandwiched between are songs with no words. There are no words for this.

I glide along Main Street, up the frozen dirt road toward the reservoir, over the mile-long earthen dam, and into the hills, jogging slow. The music sets a pace and I lean back on it, letting go of my mind.

Who knew Sooner had a death sentence, too? Hey-Soos would say, *Not destined.* Maybe not, but unavoidable because Mrs. Olsen decided to drive tired and Sooner decided to go to the restroom before he left, or argue about the bill or wait for his change, placing him on the grid that would intersect him and Ellen perfectly with Mrs. Olsen.

Who would have thought I had more time than Sooner, or Ellen Marker, for that matter? None of us will ever be too old to die young. When Mr. Cowans walked out of Mr. Phelps's office, he looked like he didn't want to live one more day. All the meanness was drained out of him. I wonder what he thought of ending Sooner's season with a broken collarbone. What are the Markers thinking over in Council? None of those people had the advantage I have. Knowing. Preparing.

I jog down out of the woods, retracing my steps, running part of the way, walking some, stopping when I have to, resting with my hands on my knees. I imagine I can feel myself slowly draining.

My God, I want to make it to the end of the year just so the student body won't fall back into that desperate hole I saw them in today.

Cody and I and Dolven and Glover and Sooner's dad and a cousin from his mom's side carry the casket at Sooner's funeral. There's not a church in town large enough to accommodate the crowd, so we use the school gym. Jocks from other schools show. There are probably more people in this gym than there are in the town.

After we bring the casket in from the hearse, Cody and the other guys and I sit with the team and Coach sits next to Mr. Cowans. I've never heard old man Cowans say a nice word to or about him, but there Coach is, hand between Boomer's shoulder blades, propping him up as if they were brothers. Sooner's mom sits quiet and stoic. Not a tear and she never takes her eyes off the casket, nor does she touch her husband. Never have I been in the presence of so much regret.

Cody taps my knee, whispers, "I can't do this, little big man." He rises, works his way past the team, and out the door. My brother has just looked to the next funeral. In the distance I think I hear him wail. This is not going to be easy. Someone else will have to help carry Sooner out. While I'm watching the door, Dallas slips into Cody's seat. She never says a word, but when the service is finished, she pats my leg and disappears.

I have no idea what that means.

Twenty-Four

It's as if Sooner kicked open the door and is holding it, waiting. Within weeks of his funeral I feel myself really slipping. Mostly it's fatigue. At times my arms and legs are too heavy to lift and this pervasive weariness almost entombs me. On days I don't make it to school, Dad stays home and lets Rance Lloyd drive the truck. Mom hasn't come out of her hole, which is bad because she's way past due. I think some part of her can't afford to watch this.

Basketball season ends, and the guys start into track. Normally this would be my time to step up as an athletic hero yet one more time; run a whole bunch of posers into the ground in the two-mile, but it's all gone. I was a little shit before, but now, little shits call me a little shit. My clothes hang on me.

Cody has signed at Boise State and they're making promises he'll start as a freshman, but he's pretty nervous. He doesn't want to do this alone. "The feather," I tell him, imitating the mouse riding in Dumbo the elephant's hat as they plummeted toward the circus tent floor when he thought he'd lost his magic feather. "It wasn't really magic! You can fly, Dumbo! Spread them ears!"

My brother will be fine. He just has to get through this time. He keeps saying maybe he'll stay a year and take care of things, as in Mom and Dad, that he was never that big on college ball anyway, but Dad would never let that happen, and that brings me peace. Dad's contract wasn't just with my mom. It was with us all. Cody will break away from me when I finally break away.

I'm living in a gauzy haze, seldom get up much now. Doc sent a hospital bed home so I can sit up and lie down at the push of a button, and I can also kill the pain any time I want. Once in a while Cody puts me in the Grey Ghost and we tool around Trout, the town we own since the Horseshoe Bend game. Coach comes over for dinner a couple of times a week. He stays until I fall asleep, then goes into Cody's room to go over hour after hour of BSU game films. Cody tells me he's getting it; it's very possible he didn't before because he didn't have to.

I want to make it to graduation. I haven't done any schoolwork for a month or more, but they've promised a social promotion if I make it. Mr. Phelps says seniors don't do any work anyway, and I'm the only honest one.

Once in a while I have a good day; one that makes Cody think I'm maybe coming back, but there are never two in a row and I'm sinking about on schedule.

It's one of those good days and I talk Cody into taking me over to Mr. Cowans's house. I've heard he hasn't come out since the funeral. I'm a little unsteady so Cody walks me up on the porch. "I'll call on my cell when I'm done," I tell him. He leaves while I knock on the door.

For a good while there's no answer, but he can't out-wait me because I've had experience with Rudy McCoy, so I pound. Finally he answers. "Hey, Mr. Cowans. Okay if I come in?"

He stands staring. I'll bet he's lost twenty-five pounds. He looks like me, for Christ sake. He doesn't answer, and he doesn't move.

"I'm coming in," I tell him and move slowly past him to the couch. He takes a deep breath, follows me inside.

I say, "Listen. I don't have much time. Or energy.

It won't be long before I'm where Sooner is."

He stares at the floor.

All I can do is tell it. "I don't know what happens next, Mr. Cowans, but I know it's something. There's a good chance I'll see Sooner. You want me to tell him anything?"

Mr. Cowans looks off to the side, runs his hand over his mouth. "Not likely you'll end up where my boy is."

"I don't think that's right, sir. I don't think God punishes you because you have. . . . " I catch myself.

So does he. "A mean old man? Well, I hope not."

"Sir, I know what happened was really hard and it wasn't fair. We all feel that way. I had warning. You didn't get any."

Nothing.

"What can I tell him, Mr. Cowans?"

He looks up with pained, dry eyes, considers me a minute, then, "Tell him I'm sorry I broke his goddamn collarbone."

I wait for more, but there isn't any, so I make my way to the porch and call my brother.

On a day when I can't tell what's real from what's not I think I see Dallas Suzuki sitting in the chair beside my bed. She's there and then she's gone and then she's there again. I don't know whether it's real or not but I don't care because my heart feels warm when I look at her and somewhere inside me, I know it's her, whether she's really here or not. Though I haven't seen Hey-Soos since I started my downward spiral, I'm starting to get it about connection, and in my weakened physical state, my spiritual state seems almost electric.

I made a deal with Coach and Mr. Phelps that if I could last I'd speak at graduation, but it ain't gonna happen. I agreed because I thought I could put a little different spin on death than the school has had following Sooner's accident. But it's a good five weeks away and I can feel myself jogging on out of here.

I have some good conscious time once or twice a day and I've been writing some things down. I'd like it if my brother talked for me. My brother can talk for me any time.

It's one of those conscious times and I'm sitting up, writing in my notebook, when I look up to see Marla, my old therapist, standing in the doorway.

I say, "Hey," and put down the notebook.

"Hey." She's tentative about walking in, but she does. "How are you?"

I smile and give her my old line. "Well, I'm dyin' but other than that. . . . "

"I came to apologize," she says, and tears nearly *squirt.* "I am *so* sorry."

"For what?"

"For leaving you. For giving up."

"Hey," I say, "you did what you had to; the oxygen mask thing, right?"

She cries harder. I do what I do best. "It's okay, Marla. I was too much of a smart-ass to do much work, anyway. . . . "

"You were dying," she says, "and I couldn't–"

"Seriously. The thing about the oxygen mask on the airplane? That's all I needed. I use it all the time. You gave me what you had."

"I left."

"Probably a pretty good thing. If it hadn't been for Dallas Suzuki, I was getting ready to put some serious transference on you. Dang, Marla. You got to pull your hair back and get some horn-rimmed glasses."

She laughs and the tears still come and she rushes over and throws her arms around my neck.

"I'm all right," I whisper into her neck. "No shit. I am. I'm doing this right."

"Forgive me?"

"No forgive to it. You were a lot better than you think. Tell you what; you go give your best to some other kid. You know, after you put on your oxygen mask and all that."

She leans back, holds me at arms' length. "I promise," she says.

"I'll be watching."

Marla hasn't been gone an hour when I look up to see the real Dallas Suzuki standing in the doorway.

"Dallas Suzuki," I say. Methinks this is my day for hot chicks.

She says, "Hi."

"Decide to give me one more chance?"

"I don't know what to say, Ben."

"Don't say anything. Just come over here and sit on this bed and let me touch you."

She sits, takes my hand, then gives a short laugh. "You're not going to try anything, are you?"

"You never know. I get these spurts."

"Ben, I'm so sorry. I was more selfish than you. I just . . . "

"I'll do the apologizing here," I say. "I should have told you."

"But–"

I drop her hand. "Shut up!"

She pulls back.

"Listen!" I tell her. "If I'd told you the truth, everything would have been fine. That's what I want to take out of here." I go back to that old thought. Something you learn on the last day of your life is as important as something you learn on the first day of grade school, because you're not dying, you're changing. And goddamn it, the truth is a powerful weapon to take into that new frontier. I can't let Dallas diminish that. "You got to let me have that."

She looks through my eyes into my soul, checking, I'm sure, to see that I mean it.

"Okay," she says.

"I'm assuming you came here to sleep with me one more time," I say.

She laughs.

"So lay your head down, 'cause I am crashing."

Dallas swings her legs around onto the bed and lays her head on my scrawny chest. I close my eyes. This is better than any sex I ever had.

Epilogue

"I was hoping I wouldn't have to do this; that my brother could deliver his own address," Cody says, looking over the darkened bleachers from the podium on the risers at the center line of the Trout High School gymnasium. "As you know we buried him a week ago. I want to thank you on behalf of my family, for your amazing kindness." He smiles. "The last thing he said to me was, 'This dyin', it ain't for sissies.'" He shakes his head. "My brother was no sissy."

He unfolds a sheet of notebook paper. "If you close your eyes," he says, "and picture me pint-size, it'll be like he's right here."

Soft laughter drifts up from the audience.

Cody reads:

"To my fellow graduates and to the citizens of Trout.

"My brother is probably pretty nervous reading this, so please laugh at his/my jokes but not at the sweat pouring off his nervous brow. That was the first joke.

"I performed a kind of forced experiment this year; one I wouldn't have chosen. Last summer Doc Wagner informed me I had a potentially terminal disease and that I should start aggressive treatment right away. Doc took me to a specialist who told me things looked bad, so I decided to forgo the treatment and give myself a reasonable shot at living a meaningful life in one year. Because I wanted that year to be 'normal', I chose to tell no one. That was a big mistake. If you don't learn anything else from my death, learn to tell the truth.

"The first time I heard the saying 'Live every day like you're going to live forever and every day like it's going to be your last' I thought it was one of those unsolvable story problems from my fifth-grade arithmetic book, but it turned out to be the truest thing about my year. When I took risks like this was my last chance and at the same time kept it in my head that my actions had consequences not only for me but for everyone I touched, forever, I made my best decisions. I did get a lot of help with that, by the way.

"It took me a while to understand, but in the end, I did my

best. I loved like I've never loved, cried like I've never cried, lived through days of terror and days of joy, days of utter satisfaction and days of shame. I shared glory on the football field I would never have experienced had I not known my fate because I wouldn't have had the nerve to try. Risk.

"Many of you may remember me only as the pain-in-the-butt Malcolm X referendum guy, and though my early poll numbers are dangerously low, I'm hoping my death will cause enough guilt that you will name a street Malcolm X Avenue. Do it.

"I spent the year anticipating my impending demise. There were times I was paralyzed with fear but in the end I'm glad I knew. Another of our classmates, Sooner Cowans, is also gone—with no warning—and I have to say I'm grateful I had the chance to make my peace. Rest assured that, by the time you hear this, I've already found him and told him he is loved and missed—which he already knows—that we are out here throwing the ball around, our earthly differences dwarfed by the vast and glorious universe, creating eight-man plays so clever and intricate we could kick Timberline's butt on ten Friday afternoons out of ten.

"So, graduating seniors, remember you can keep us alive on Earth with the acts you perform in our names. Decide for yourselves how to do that for Sooner, but for me, I want my

Malcolm X Avenue. And by the way, Sooner says his street would be the right one to carry that name.

"Drive carefully."

Cody folds the paper and wipes his eyes as a light applause turns thunderous.

Cody Wolf and Dallas Suzuki jog easily along the reservoir road exactly two weeks following their high school graduation. Joe Henry Suzuki rides ahead of Dallas in a jogger's stroller, the wind blowing his fine black hair straight back.

"Your son, huh?" Cody says.

"Yeah. Isn't he beautiful?"

"Yeah, isn't I beautiful?" Joe Henry says.

"That you are, big boy," Cody says back. "That you are. Stick your fingers in your ears and go 'Ahhhhhhhhhhhhhhhh' for as long as you can."

Joe Henry bites.

Over his noise, Cody says, "It took a lot of guts to up and tell the world. I mean, your uncle and everything."

"It was killing me," Dallas says.

"I'll bet."

Joe Henry demonstrates powerful lungs, "Ahhhhhhhhhhhhh."

"You gonna be able to play volleyball and take care of him, too?"

"I'll find a way. Have to. No volleyball scholarship, no school. No school, the little prince here grows up in a double wide."

"Can't believe we both got scholarships to the same place," Cody says through increasingly heavy breathing. "Listen, I've been thinking. Why don't we get a place together? No strings. Between us I bet we could cover the bases for this little snot factory."

Dallas still breathes easily, almost gliding as she pushes Joe Henry toward the bluff overlooking the reservoir. "I'll think about it." They run another hundred yards. "I'll bet Ben would like that."

They run in silence, save for Cody's gasps for oxygen, to the top of the bluff, where Dallas takes Ben's iPod from the pocket on the back of the stroller, finds song 116, listens a moment and hands Cody one of the earphones:

So I will climb the highest hill
And I'll watch the rising sun
And pray that I won't feel the chill
'Til I'm too old to die young.

Let me watch my children grow
To see what they become
Lord don't let that cold wind blow
'Til I'm too old to die young.

They watch till the sun sits atop a western peak, then turn and head back for town. Cody is hugely appreciative that the rest of the run is mostly downhill.

They jog easily past the Cowanses, home, dark but for the blue glow of the television screen through the living room window. At the end of the street, beneath a handmade plywood street sign reading MALCOLM X AVENUE, they split and jog to their separate homes.